Between Sky and Surface

(A Chrysalis Kaleidoscope Novel)

By: Nathan Parker

Table of Contents

Prologue

In the vastness of the desert, an expanse so vast and so
relentless, it seemed to stretch into eternity, where
each grain of sand held the weight of untold stories,
whispered secrets to the wind as if in prayer. The sun, a
relentless sovereign, cast its unyielding gaze upon the
earth, ruling the sky with a life-giving and life-taking
brilliance. Amidst this realm of endless gold and
blistering heat, a lone figure emerged as a silhouette
against the blinding light, standing as still as the ancient
rocks that framed the horizon, monuments to time
itself.

This figure, a solitary sentinel amidst the desolation,
seemed almost a mirage, a trick of the light or perhaps a
phantom conjured by the heat. Yet, the occasional
flicker of eyes, sharp and observant, betrayed a
vigilance that was all too real. These eyes, piercing and
unblinking, tracked the slow but determined approach
of three humans: a man, worn by the journey yet
unbowed; a woman, her strength evident in the set of
her shoulders and the determination in her gaze; and a
baby, cradled gently in the woman's arms, innocent to
the harshness of the world it was born into.

The trio moved with a purpose that spoke of
desperation and hope intertwined. Their steps were
measured, leaving a transient mark upon the sand, a

testament to their passage. The desert around them was alive with the sounds of their struggle: the soft scuff of their feet against the sand, the labored breaths that spoke of exhaustion, and the gentle cooing of the baby, oblivious to the monumental journey it was a part of.

As they drew nearer, the figure's presence became more pronounced, an anchor in the shifting landscape. The air around them seemed to thrum with a palpable tension, the moment suspended as if both time and nature held their breath in anticipation. For all its vastness and indifference, the desert became a stage upon which a pivotal scene was about to unfold, a crossroads that would alter the course of their lives in ways they could scarcely imagine.

The sun, now dipping towards the horizon, painted the sky in hues of fire and gold, casting long shadows that danced upon the sand, mingling with the silhouettes of the approaching family and the enigmatic figure awaiting them. In this liminal space, where day met night and the elements of earth, air, and fire converged, their fates were poised to intertwine, guided by ancient forces and the whispered secrets of the desert wind.

The desert stood still in its vast and merciless sprawl, a momentary cessation in its timeless march under the sun. The relentless expanse of heat and emptiness, constantly shifting, always whispering, seemed to pause as if the sands were holding their breath. The trio, a small beacon of life amid this endless sea of solitude, made their final steps toward the lone figure, their resolve as palpable as the heat that shimmered in the air around them. It was as though their journey, marked by each painstaking step through the sand, had led them to this singular point in time and space, where destiny awaited their arrival.

Now thick with anticipation, the air seemed to quiver with the weight of their purpose. It carried their voices forward, slicing through the silence that enveloped the desert, a silence that had borne witness to countless sunrises and sunsets, unchanging yet ever-watchful. When they finally spoke, their words cut through the stillness, an invocation of sorts, calling upon the mysteries that lay beyond.

"We seek the Island," the man declared, his voice a steady beacon amidst the swirling sands of uncertainty. Despite the evident toll of their journey, his words carried a strength and clarity that resonated in the air. It was a statement of intent, of need, born from a place of deep yearning and propelled by the hope of finding refuge, a new beginning in a world far removed from the harsh embrace of the desert.

His companions stood in silent affirmation, the woman with a look of unwavering determination, the baby unaware of the magnitude of the moment yet central to their plea. Their collective presence, united in purpose and bolstered by their bond, emanated a sense of urgency and hope. They were seekers at the threshold of an unseen world, petitioners at the door of fate, asking to be granted passage to a realm spoken of in whispers and dreams—the Island, a place of legend and promise, suspended above the grasp of the world they knew, a haven floating in the sky, untouched by the desolation that surrounded them.

Their declaration, simple yet profound, hung between them and the figure. It was a request that bridged worlds, a plea for acceptance into a sanctuary that seemed as distant as the stars. At this moment, the vastness of the desert, with all its cruelty and beauty, became a mere backdrop to the human drama unfolding, a testament to the resilience of those who dare to dream amidst the desolation.

The figure enshrouded in the enigmatic shadows cast by the waning sun, stood as an unmoving testament to the solemnity of the moment. This silent guardian, a mere silhouette against the backdrop of the desert's vast canvas, seemed to be carved from the very essence of the landscape itself—timeless, inscrutable, and imposing. The air around them, already thick with the anticipation of the trio's plea, grew denser as if charged with the gravity of their request. This sentinel, a keeper of the threshold between the barren earth and the utopian sanctuary above, assessed their worth from a distance beyond physical; it was a chasm spanned by courage, hope, and the desperate human need for belonging.

"Why do you approach?" The voice that broke the silence did not seem to come directly from the figure but rather from the atmosphere that enveloped them, as if the desert had found a voice. Ageless, resonating with the weight of centuries, it seemed to echo from the sands to the sky, a question that was both an invitation and a challenge.

The woman, undeterred by the formality of the inquiry, drew the baby closer to her heart, an instinctive gesture of protection and assertion. Her response, spoken with a clarity and conviction that cut through the oppressive heat, belied the physical exhaustion that marked her features. "We believe our addition to the Island would be beneficial. We bring skills and knowledge, and this child, born of a world below but destined for the skies." Her voice, imbued with the strength of her conviction, carried a plea for sanctuary and a promise—a vow that their presence within the Island's domain would not be in vain.

Her words, spoken on behalf of the trio, were more than just an answer; they were a declaration of intent and potential. The skills and knowledge she spoke of were not merely practical assets but symbols of their willingness to contribute and weave their lives into the fabric of the Island's society. The child cradled so tenderly in her arms represented hope for their future and the continuation of a legacy that transcended the harsh realities of the world below—a beacon of potential that, in their eyes, was destined to soar amidst the clouds.

This assertion of their value, delivered with an unwavering belief in their worthiness and the child's destined greatness, hung in the balance as they awaited the figure's judgment. Their fate, and that of the child destined for the skies, now rested in the hands of this sentinel, the guardian of the path to a new life among the clouds.

Their plea uttered with a blend of desperation and optimism, lingered in the air like a delicate wisp of smoke, a fragile hope dancing amidst the vast desolation of the desert. The figure, an enigmatic silhouette against the canvas of the arid landscape, remained unmoved in demeanor. A stoic observer of the human drama unfolding before them, the figure seemed to draw the threads of their words into a tapestry of consideration, the silence that stretched between them akin to the infinite expanse of the desert stretching to the distant horizon.

The trio, still as statues, watched the figure with bated breath, suspended in the uncertain space between plea and judgment, and time slowed its march as if hesitant to move forward, allowing the moment's weight to settle upon the shifting sands. The desert, an indifferent witness to countless tales of triumph and despair, stood as a silent theater for the unfolding destiny of those who dared to seek refuge in the Island suspended above.

Then, with a grace that mirrored the fluidity of the desert winds, the figure turned. The cloak billowed in the late afternoon breeze, a transient dance before it settled into the formless shadows. The figure vanished as if swallowed by the landscape it inhabited, leaving only the echoes of their presence behind.

In the wake of this mysterious departure, a stunned silence hung heavy in the air. The trio, their eyes fixed on the spot where the figure once stood, felt the weight of anticipation lift, replaced by a profound uncertainty. What judgment had been rendered, and what awaited them after this encounter?

As if responding to an unseen cue, the ground beneath the trio began to stir. The very earth seemed to awaken, trembling in response to forces beyond the comprehension of mere mortals. In this moment of collective astonishment, the sands shifted, revealing an ancient and mystical secret hidden beneath the surface.

A platform known only to those initiated into the ancient ways of the desert rose from the sands. A manifestation of both the mysticism and practicality that governed the unseen realms, the platform announced its purpose with unwavering clarity. It was a conduit between worlds, a bridge from the desolation of the desert to the promised sanctuary in the sky— how the trio's destiny would be fulfilled. As if guided by an invisible hand, the platform awaited their ascent, a vessel for their journey from the realm of sand to the ethereal heights where the Island awaited.

With a shared glance transcending spoken words, the family communicated a silent agreement, a pact forged in the crucible of adversity. Their eyes, reflecting the ardent flicker of hope, spoke of new beginnings and the courage to embrace the unknown. The trio, bound by blood and the shared burden of dreams, approached the mystical platform with a reverence reserved for the sacred. Each step, a testament to their unwavering determination, echoed through the stillness of the desert, a prelude to the forthcoming ascent into a realm suspended between earth and sky.

As they stepped onto the platform, the sands beneath their feet seemed to sigh in relief, as if acknowledging the departure of those whose destinies were now entwined with the promise of the floating Island. The platform, responding to the weight of their collective resolve, stirred to life, its ascent a testament to the ancient forces that governed its existence.

Rising above the undulating dunes, the platform carried them toward the heavens, leaving behind the vast expanse of the desert that had both tested and witnessed their journey. The family, silhouetted against the backdrop of the fading sun, held on to each other, a human anchor amid the ethereal ascent. The baby, cradled in the woman's arms, seemed to gaze at the receding desert with innocent curiosity, unaware of the profound significance of the voyage it was part of.

As the platform ascended, the desert below began to reclaim its stillness as if absorbing the echoes of their departure. Once disturbed by the trio's footsteps, the sands settled into an undisturbed repose, returning to the timeless rhythm of the desert. The whispering winds, the only witnesses to the family's departure, carried the echoes of a plea, a response, and the promise of a new chapter yet to be written.

Meanwhile, above the clouds and hidden within their veiled embrace, the Island awaited. A realm suspended in the sky held the promise of peace above the world's turmoil below. Secrets, ancient and profound, danced within the clouds, and destinies were shrouded in the mist that veiled the floating sanctuary. The Island, a beacon of sanctuary, stood as a guardian of dreams and a keeper of untold truths, poised to welcome those seeking refuge in its celestial embrace. The family, carried by the mystical ascent, embarked on a journey toward a future untold, guided by the unseen currents of fate and the whispers of a world veiled in clouds.

Part 1: The Shadow's Whisper

Chapter 1: The Ceremony of Bonds

Beneath the floating Island, concealed within the labyrinthine caves adorned with shimmering crystals, the Ceremony of Bonds unfolded in an atmosphere humming with ancient magic. The air within the cavern seemed to shimmer with tangible energy as if the walls themselves held the echoes of countless ceremonies that had transpired in the womb of this subterranean sanctuary. The soft luminescence from the crystals, nestled intricately in the cave's natural formations, painted the space in hues that defied earthly descriptions. These were not mere rocks; they were conduits of the Island's essence, each crystal a repository of the magic that coursed through the veins of the floating land above.

As the residents gathered, their anticipation hung like a delicate mist, blending seamlessly with the otherworldly glow. The elders, draped in ceremonial robes adorned with symbols of ancient wisdom, positioned themselves strategically within the cavern's embrace. The melody of their chants, a melodic invocation passed down through generations, reverberated through the hollows, reaching the depths where the Island's heartbeat was in harmony with its chosen inhabitants.

The grandeur of the cave, a tapestry of shadow and light, served as a testament to the sacredness of the

Ceremony of Bonds. It was a space where the mundane transcended into the mystical, where the threads of fate intertwined with the fabric of the Island's existence. The crystals, now pulsating in synchrony with the elders' chants, cast ethereal patterns upon the ground, creating a mesmerizing dance of shadows that mirrored the profound interplay of magic and destiny.

The Ceremony of Bonds, a fusion of mysticism and tradition, bridged the tangible and the intangible. As Tiriaq moved further into the cave, the luminescent glow intensified, casting elongated shadows that danced upon the walls. The convergence of magic reached its zenith, and the cavern seemed to exhale, releasing the accumulated energy into the sacred space.

Amid this cosmic ballet, the residents, each a participant in the intricate choreography of the ceremony, felt the resonance of a force beyond comprehension. The very walls of the cave held the secrets of a lineage written in the language of crystals, a history that whispered through the stones and reverberated through the souls of those who dared to venture into its depths.

The Ceremony of Bonds, a celestial dialogue between the Island and its residents, continued its enchanting symphony. The residents, bound by the shared hope and expectation, witnessed the magic unfurling around them. The cave, an aperture to the Island's mystical core, became a sacred theater where destinies were inscribed, where the bonds forged within its embrace would ripple through time like echoes in the cavern's expanse.

Tiriaq, a figure of contrast against the radiant backdrop, stood at the entrance of the grand cavern, the luminescence casting an ethereal glow upon his features. The elders commenced their chant, a harmonious symphony resonating with the very heartbeat of the Island. Around Tiriaq, his classmates, adorned in ceremonial attire, shared the anticipation on his face. As the elders' voices intertwined with the ambient magic, the cavern transformed into a kaleidoscope of hues, the crystals responding to the Island's energy.

Encouraged by the pulsating melody, Tiriaq, and his peers walked further into the cavern, where the glow of the crystals became the sole source of illumination. The air, thick with ancient enchantment, grew denser as they ventured deeper. The radiant luminescence that once revealed the intricacies of the cave began to wane, surrendering to the looming darkness that enveloped them. Shadows clung to the walls like specters, and the kaleidoscope of colors gradually dissolved into a sea of obsidian.

Tiriaq strained his eyes to discern the shapes around him, the once vivid hues now reduced to subtle glimmers. While still palpable, the ambient magic manifested as a gentle hum rather than a vibrant display. His classmates, their ceremonial attire mere silhouettes in the encroaching darkness, moved with a shared purpose through the cavern's narrow passages.

The elders' intertwining voices guided them like a celestial compass, the harmonic resonance leading them deeper into the heart of the cave. Now calm and mysterious, the air carried the scent of ancient secrets. As the cavern's embrace tightened, the anticipation etched on Tiriaq's face became a blend of wonder and trepidation. His classmates, too, exchanged glances, their expressions navigating the thin line between awe and uncertainty.

In this realm where the luminescent glow faltered, Tiriaq's gaze sought Ayuka's silhouette, now a mere outline in the diminishing light. Their connection, shared history, and childhood memories lingered in obscurity. The camaraderie forged in the anticipation of the ceremony solidified their unity, even as the encroaching darkness threatened to shroud their familiar faces.

As they ventured further, the symphony of the elders' chants enveloped them like a cocoon, providing a fragile reassurance in the face of the deepening obscurity. The labyrinthine passages, now indistinct in the darkness, seemed to echo with the footsteps of those who had walked this path before, an ancestral chorus that added to the mystique of the Ceremony of Bonds.

The Ceremony of Bonds, a communion between the Island and its residents, was a dance of fate and magic, an ancient choreography that echoed through the very soul of the cavern. It was a manifestation of the Island's essence, an ethereal ballet where destiny and the mystical intertwined, leaving an indelible mark on the tapestry of time. In this sacred rite, familiars, as manifestations of the Island's essence, embarked on a dance of their own, choosing companions from among the hopeful residents. Each bond, a sacred agreement etched in the language of magic, was an unspoken pact that resonated through the cavern's depths and reverberated through the generations that would follow.

Amid the ritual's crescendo, a figure emerged from the shadows—a Lion familiar, its silhouette a majestic presence against the darkness that now enveloped the cave. The Lion, a creature of both strength and subtlety, moved with regal grace, its form an embodiment of the Island's ancient power. Tiriaq, ensnared in the enchantment of the moment, felt the warmth of the creature's ethereal presence enveloping him like a comforting shroud. The Lion's mane, aglow with a luminosity that defied the dimness, seemed to capture the very essence of the ceremony.

As Tiriaq's eyes locked onto the Lion's, a connection unfolded in the crucible of destiny, a meeting of souls bound by the unseen threads of fate. Witnessing countless such unions, the cavern held its breath in anticipation as the Lion, guided by the Island's wisdom, approached Tiriaq with a regality that echoed through the ages. The air, thick with the resonance of the elders' chants, crackled with the intensity of the bond forming before their eyes. The Lion's eyes, pools of ancient wisdom, met Tiriaq's with a knowing gaze, acknowledging the weight of the role bestowed upon him.

In this moment of mystical convergence, Tiriaq and the Lion stood as symbols of unity, their destinies intertwined in a dance that transcended the physical and delved into the very essence of existence. The Lion, a guardian chosen by the Island, had found its companion in Tiriaq, a resident poised at the threshold of leadership. The Ceremony of Bonds, an immortal ballet performed in the cave's timeless stage, had once again woven a tale of connection and purpose that would echo through the annals of the Island's history.

As the residents dispersed, a buzz of excitement filled the cavern. Ayuka, a fellow resident, had also bonded with a Lion, her silhouette glimpsed amidst the crowd.

The ceremony's aftermath was a swirling dance of elation and camaraderie, with residents exchanging smiles and sharing the euphoria of their newfound bonds. Yet, in the ebb and flow of the ceremony's aftermath, Tiriaq and Ayuka lost track of each other amidst the shifting sea of jubilant residents.

The cavern, once vibrant with the magic of the Ceremony of Bonds, echoed with the footsteps and laughter of those who had forged connections with their familiars. Ayuka's silhouette, barely discernible in the shadows, became a fleeting memory in the tapestry of the communal experience. The whispers of shared excitement and animated conversations melded into a harmonious chorus that resonated through the cavern's expanse.

Only when Tiriaq stepped out into the daylight, the brilliance of the Island above unfolding before him did the realization dawn upon him. The luminescent glow of the crystals outside the cave bathed the landscape in an otherworldly radiance. In the clarity of the sunlit world, the grandeur of the Island revealed itself, suspended in the sky like a celestial haven. Yet, as Tiriaq marveled at the breathtaking sight, a subtle unease began to gnaw at the edges of his joy.

In the embrace of daylight, he felt the coexistence of strength and subtlety within his familiar. The Lion, wreathed in Shadow, was not merely a manifestation of power but a harbinger of complexity and duality. The realization descended upon Tiriaq like a shadow cast upon his newfound sense of purpose. The warmth he had felt in the cavern now mingled with an apprehension that clung to him like a whisper in the wind.

The Lion, a creature of majesty and darkness, bore a terrible portend that loomed over Tiriaq's life. As he gazed at the brilliant expanse of the Island above, he couldn't shake the haunting feeling that his journey, now intertwined with the enigmatic Lion, was destined to unfold amidst the delicate balance between strength and subtlety, light and shadow. The brilliance of the Island's skies above concealed the mysteries that awaited Tiriaq, and the Lion, a creature of obscurity, stood as a silent guardian of the secrets veiled within the floating sanctuary.

Chapter 2: Exile

The days following the Ceremony of Bonds were tainted with an unspoken tension that lingered over the Island like a shroud. Tiriaq, now bonded to the enigmatic Lion, discovered that his familiar bore an unusual duality— the Lion of both majesty and Shadow. As the Island's residents began to discern the truth, confusion, and concern rippled through the once-close-knit community.

The enchantment of the Ceremony of Bonds, once a celebration of unity and shared destinies, had given way to a disquieting undercurrent. The Island, suspended in its celestial sanctuary, now grappled with the revelation that the harmony they had cherished was threatened by a discordant note—a Shadow familiar, an omen of upheaval.

Tiriaq's presence became a focal point for the residents, his every step shadowed by a gaze that wavered between curiosity and apprehension. Former friends exchanged hushed conversations, their once-open expressions now guarded. The enchanting glow that bathed the floating structures seemed dimmed as if the revelation had tempered the very magic of the Island.

Like the rustle of leaves before a gathering storm, whispers followed Tiriaq wherever he went. The Lion, a creature embodying both majesty and the ominous hint of shadow, walked beside him as a silent companion, its presence casting a mysterious aura that stirred emotions ranging from awe to fear.

The shift in Tiriaq's social landscape was as swift as harsh. A chasm of uncertainty and fear now replaced the camaraderie and companionship that had defined his relationships. The shadows that danced around his Lion, a spectacle that once might have been celebrated as a marvel of the Island's magical diversity, now cast a pall over Tiriaq's interactions. Friends who had shared laughter and dreams under the vast, starlit skies now crossed to the other side of the path when they saw him approaching, their gazes fixed on the horizon as if the very sight of him and his shadow-wreathed companion might bring misfortune.

The markets, bustling centers of trade and gossip, became gauntlets for Tiriaq to run through. The hushed tones of the merchants, the sidelong glances, and the sudden silences as he passed told a story of a community grappling with fear. Even the children, usually impervious to the complexities of adult apprehensions, seemed to sense the shift. Their innocent questions about his Lion met with hurried shushing from their elders.

This isolation extended into the very heart of his daily life. Where once Tiriaq was a beloved figure, effortlessly blending into the fabric of communal gatherings, he now found himself on the periphery, a specter at the feast. Invitations dwindled, and the casual, open-door welcomes that were the Island's hallmark became less forthcoming. In their place stood a barrier invisible but palpable, erected not from stone or spell but from suspicion and the primal fear of the unknown.

Despite the growing estrangement, there were moments when the old warmth seemed about to break through the frost. Yet, each time, the sight of the Lion, its majestic form cloaked in undulating shadows, seemed to reinforce the walls between Tiriaq and his community. Once a source of pride, the Lion's presence now served as a constant reminder of the divide, a gulf that widened with every step they took together through the winding streets and airy plazas of their floating world.

Tiriaq's family, transplanted to the Island years ago for the peace and magic it promised, now found themselves at the heart of a storm they had never anticipated. Once filled with the light laughter of shared stories and the warmth of communal meals, their home had taken on a somber atmosphere. The revelation of Tiriaq's bond with a Shadow familiar—a phenomenon unheard of in recent memory—cast a long shadow over their daily lives. Despite the growing unease outside their doors, within the walls of their dwelling, Tiriaq was met with an unyielding fortress of familial love and support.

His parents, adept in the lore and legends of their new home, poured over ancient texts and whispered secrets, seeking to understand the nature of Tiriaq's bond. They shared with him the stories of the Shadow familiar, tales of when the Island was young, and magic was a wild, untamed force. These stories passed down through generations, hinted at the duality of magic— the light and the dark—and the role of the Shadow familiar in balancing these forces. Yet, they also spoke of a prophecy that foretold an End to the Island's Peace, a prophecy now intertwined with Tiriaq's fate.

Tiriaq's siblings stood by him, their bond unshaken by the whispers and wary glances that followed their brother. They became his confidants, sharing in his moments of doubt and bolstering his spirits with their unwavering belief in him. Together, they explored the depths of the familiar's magic, testing its limits and discovering its nuances. With its majestic form and enigmatic aura, the Lion became less a source of fear and more a symbol of the unknown potential within Tiriaq.

Yet, beneath their support, a current of worry ran deep. Tiriaq could see it in the furrowed brows of his parents as they discussed in hushed tones long into the night, in the way their hands lingered over his shoulders a moment too long as if to reassure both themselves and him that they were still united. They worried about the implications of the prophecy, about what it meant for their son and the life they had built on the Island. They worried about the growing distance between their family and the rest of the community, about the isolation that seemed to grow with each passing day.

Despite these challenges, Tiriaq's family remained his sanctuary, a beacon of hope in a sea of uncertainty. They reminded him that, though the path ahead was shrouded in shadow, he would not walk it alone. Together, they faced the future, determined to uncover the truth of the Shadow familiar and to find a way to protect the peace of the Island they had come to call home.

The revelation of Ayuka's bond with the Golden familiar was met with an outpouring of admiration and hope across the Island. Her newfound connection symbolized prosperity and protection, starkly contrasting the ambiguity and fear that shrouded Tiriaq's bond. As word of her bonding spread like wildfire through their home's floating structures and verdant pathways, Ayuka was thrust into the limelight, her every move watched with eager eyes, and her every word weighed for its potential to inspire and lead.

The Golden Familiar, a creature of myth and legend, was known to the Islanders for its radiant beauty and formidable power. It was said to embody the very essence of the Island's magic, a guardian of light and harbinger of peace. Thus, Ayuka's bond with such a being sparked a wave of pride among the residents, who saw in her a beacon of hope in uncertain times. Families recounted tales of the Golden Familiar's past appearances, each story embellished with the victories and prosperity that followed. The community's elders spoke of ancient prophecies that foretold the return of the Golden Familiar in a time of need, reinforcing the belief that Ayuka and her majestic companion were destined to lead the Island into a new era of peace and stability.

This burgeoning pride in Ayuka's bond created an unintended chasm within the community. On one side were those who rallied behind her, their faith in her ability to protect and guide the Island unwavering. They saw her as a unifying force, a symbol of the strength and resilience of their society. Gatherings and discussions often centered around the potential of her newfound powers and how they could be harnessed for the good of all.

On the other side, however, were those whose focus turned toward the shadow that now accompanied

Tiriaq. The stark contrast between the light of Ayuka's Golden familiar and the darkness of Tiriaq's Shadow lion deepened the divide, fueling fears and superstitions. This segment of the community viewed the shadow with suspicion and unease, worried about the implications of its presence and the ancient prophecy that hinted at turmoil and change. Conversations whispered in the corners of communal spaces often pondered whether the appearance of the Shadow familiar signaled a threat to the peace and balance of their Island.

Despite the growing divide, Ayuka did not subscribe to the fears that shadowed Tiriaq's presence. She remembered the boy she grew up with, the friend she knew before fate marked them with bonds of contrasting natures. In her heart, Ayuka harbored no belief that Tiriaq posed a danger to their community. This conviction placed her at odds with the prevailing sentiment, challenging her to navigate the delicate balance between embracing her role as a protector and defending the friend she still saw in Tiriaq.

As the Island grappled with these contrasting emotions, the community stood at a crossroads, torn between the light and the shadow, between the past and the uncertain promise of the future. Amid this turmoil, Ayuka and Tiriaq found themselves at the heart of a prophecy that could either unite their world or tear it apart.

Ayuka's stance on Tiriaq and his Shadow familiar placed her in a unique, often isolating position within the community. While others viewed Tiriaq with suspicion and sometimes outright fear, Ayuka remembered the boy who laughed freely under the sunlit skies, who shared dreams beside the whispering tides. This Tiriaq, the one touched by shadow, was still the same person at heart, she believed. Her conviction stemmed not from naivety but from a deep understanding of the essence of bonds—those formed by friendship were as significant as those formed with familiars.

Despite her efforts to communicate this perspective, Ayuka lost her words amidst the whirlwind of concern and speculation that now defined the community's discourse. The residents once unified in their traditions and celebrations, now harbored a collective unease that seemed to cloud their judgment. The essence of their society, built on trust and mutual respect, appeared to be eroding under fear. Conversations that once revolved around cooperation and communal success were now tainted by whispers of caution and the need for vigilance.

This shift was particularly painful for Ayuka. She witnessed firsthand how the bonds of community were strained, how suspicion crept into interactions that were once marked by openness and warmth. The duality of her position—as both the chosen companion of the Golden familiar and a defender of Tiriaq's character—required a delicate balance that was increasingly difficult to maintain as the island's atmosphere grew more charged.

Ayuka's assurances, her attempts to bridge the growing divide with stories of their shared past, and her belief in Tiriaq's inherent goodness often felt like trying to hold back the tide with open hands. The more she spoke of unity and understanding, the more she sensed the undercurrent of fear pulling at the fabric of their community. It was a fear of the unknown and the potential for change that the Shadow familiar represented. To many, Tiriaq's bond was a harbinger of upheaval, challenging the status quo and forcing a confrontation with deeply held beliefs and fears.

In her quiet moments, Ayuka grappled with the weight of her role and the realization that her voice, vital though it might be, was not enough to quell the rising tide of apprehension alone. She understood that the path forward was not through words alone but actions that could demonstrate the true nature of her conviction. The challenge lay in navigating the delicate dynamics of her community, finding a way to protect without alienating, to lead without dictating, and most importantly, to heal the fractures that threatened to undo the fabric of their shared lives on the Island.

The chamber where the elders convened was a place of deep spiritual significance, its walls echoing with the wisdom of ages past. Here, under the solemn gaze of ancestral spirits immortalized in the myriad tapestries that adorned the stone, the council of elders sought guidance. The air was thick with the scent of burning incense, symbolizing their plea for clarity and wisdom from the forces that watched over the Island.

At the center of their circle, an ancient artifact called the Heartstone pulsed with a soft, ethereal light. It was said that the Heartstone's glow mirrored the health of the Island, its luminescence a testament to the harmony that prevailed. But now, its light flickered uncertainly as if troubled by the same concerns that weighed heavily on the elders' hearts.

The discussion was tense, each elder acutely aware of the stakes. The prophecy, long regarded as a mere legend, spoke of a time when the Island would stand on the brink of upheaval, ushered in by the emergence of a Shadow familiar. This familiar, the prophecy warned, would be both a test and a turning point for the Island's people, challenging the very foundations of their way of life.

"Some may argue we are too hasty," Elder Marnik, the council's most venerable member, began his voice a low rumble that seemed to resonate with the stone itself. "But we do not have the luxury of time. The Heartstone's unrest is a sign that we cannot ignore. The prophecy is clear—our peace and existence may depend on our actions now."

Another elder, Sarnia, known for her wisdom and measured approach, countered, "Yet, must our action be so severe? Exile is a sentence we have not imposed for generations. To cast out one of our own, especially one so young and untested..."

Her voice trailed off, the unspoken implication hanging heavily in the air. It was not just Tiriaq who would be affected by this decision but the entire fabric of their community, woven together by bonds of trust and mutual support.

Elder Jorun, a stern figure with a keen strategic mind, added, "Our priority is the safety and harmony of the Island. The prophecy does not merely suggest but warns of the Shadow's potential to unravel what we have so painstakingly built. Exile, though a harsh measure, may indeed be our only recourse to prevent a greater calamity."

The debate continued, with each elder bringing forth their insights, fears, and hopes for the Island's future. The decision to consider exile was not made lightly; it was a testament to the depth of their concern for the well-being of their community. The elders understood that their responsibility was not just to the present but to the future generations who would inherit the Island.

As the deliberation drew to a close, a heavy silence settled over the chamber. The Heartstone's light, still uncertain, cast long shadows across the faces of the elders. It was a visual reminder of the difficult path they were poised to choose—a path that could alter the course of their history.

The final decision, sealed with a collective, albeit heavy-hearted agreement, was to prepare for the possibility of exile. The elders would seek Tiriaq out, offering him a chance to understand the gravity of his situation and the reasons behind their grave considerations. It was a decision born not out of malice but out of a deep-seated duty to protect the Island and its people from a fate the prophecy had ominously foretold.

In the dimly lit recesses of the council chamber, where the air was thick with the weight of centuries, the elders leaned closer, their voices a mere whisper against the backdrop of the Heartstone's unsettling flicker. The ancient and ominous prophecy had been passed down through generations, its words etched into the very soul of the Island's keepers. It spoke of a time when the balance between light and shadow would be threatened, a period of upheaval initiated by the bond between a resident and a Shadow familiar.

"This Shadow familiar," Elder Marnik murmured, his eyes reflecting the troubled light of the Heartstone, "it is said to be both a part and apart from the Island, a creature of deep magic, bound to the fate of our people. Its emergence is a sign, a warning of trials to come, of a darkness that could engulf us all."

The details of the prophecy were not recorded in any book or scroll but carried in the oral traditions of the elders, a sacred trust that demanded both reverence and caution. Each elder held a piece of the story, a fragment of the larger tapestry portraying the Island's history and potential future.

Elder Sarnia, her voice steady but soft, added, "And yet, the prophecy also speaks of choice, of paths that might lead us away from the darkness. The Shadow familiar is not merely an omen of despair but a test of our resolve, our unity. We must tread carefully, for to act in fear is already succumbing to the shadows we seek to evade."

The room fell silent, the weight of their responsibility pressing down upon them. The decision to consider exile for Tiriaq was not just a reaction to the immediate fear his bond invoked but a complex calculation of risks and outcomes influenced by the prophecy's dire warnings. The Shadow familiar, intertwined with Tiriaq's fate, was now a pivotal figure in the unfolding drama of the Island's destiny.

Elder Jorun, known for his pragmatic approach, voiced the concern that lingered unspoken in the minds of his peers. "If the prophecy is to be our guide, then we must also consider its implications for unity and division. To exile Tiriaq is to send a message to our people, one that might sow further seeds of fear and mistrust. Are we prepared to face the consequences of our actions, not just today, but for the legacy we leave for future generations?"

The debate that followed was a delicate dance of logic, emotion, and intuition as the elders grappled with the prophecy's unknowns and the genuine challenges it presented. They were custodians of the Island's past and architects of its future, a role that demanded both wisdom and courage.

As the meeting drew to a close, the decision to move forward with the possibility of exile was made with heavy hearts. With its veiled warnings and cryptic messages, the prophecy remained a specter over their deliberations, a reminder of the fragile balance they were sworn to protect. In their quest to avert the darkness foretold, the elders committed themselves to a path fraught with uncertainty, hoping against hope that their actions would safeguard the Island's peace for generations to come.

In the somber silence of the council chamber, where the walls themselves seemed to absorb the moment's gravity, Tiriaq faced the assembly of elders. Their aged faces, etched with the wisdom and burdens of their roles, formed a semi-circle around him, a tableau of solemn judgment. The air was heavy, with the palpable tension of destiny being irrevocably altered.

Tiriaq, his posture defiant yet underscored by a palpable undercurrent of isolation, listened as the verdict of his future was unveiled. The elders spoke not with anger but with a tone of regret, their words laced with an ancient sorrow that transcended the immediate predicament. They recounted the essence of the prophecy, its veiled warnings, and the unprecedented nature of his bond with the Shadow familiar. This creature, a being of both darkness and light, had become the fulcrum upon which the Island's fate now teetered.

"The balance of our world," Elder Anara began, her voice steady but tinged with an undeniable sadness, "has been maintained through harmony between the seen and unseen, light and shadow. While extraordinary, your bond with the Shadow familiar threatens to tip this balance, inviting the chaos foretold in the prophecy."

Tiriaq's gaze met each of their eyes, searching for an ally among them, a glimmer of understanding or perhaps a shadow of doubt. But he found a unified front, a collective resolve born out of the fear of what might come to pass if the prophecy's warnings were ignored.

With a sigh that seemed to carry the weight of the world, Elder Goren added, "It is with heavy hearts that we conclude your continued presence among us risks the very peace we have sworn to protect. While not of your choosing, your bond with the Shadow familiar has entwined you with a destiny that endangers all we hold dear."

The chamber echoed with the solemnity of their decree. Tiriaq, now the embodiment of a feared prophecy, was to be exiled from the Island, severed from the community and the life he had known. The elders believed that removing him could avert the darkness that loomed on the horizon, preserving the Island's tranquility.

As Tiriaq absorbed the finality of their decision, a surge of emotions overwhelmed him—anger, disbelief, and a profound sense of betrayal. The Island, his home, its residents, his family, and his friends were now lost to him, all because of an ancient text and the fear it instilled.

The elders, their expressions a complex tapestry of duty, sorrow, and unwavering conviction, offered him words of comfort, hollow in the face of the exile they imposed. They spoke of the possibility of redemption, of a future where the prophecy's shadows might be dispelled, allowing for his return. But to Tiriaq, these words were little more than whispers against the storm within him.

As he turned to leave, the weight of their judgment pressing down upon him, Tiriaq realized the journey ahead would be one of solitude and survival. The Shadow familiar, his unwitting companion in exile, was now his only ally in a world that had turned its back on him. The path forward was unclear, fraught with uncertainty and danger, but it was a path he must walk alone, guided by the faint hope that one day he might prove the prophecy wrong and reclaim his place among his people.

As Tiriaq stepped out of the council chamber, the weight of the elders' judgment settled like an unshakable shroud upon his shoulders. The once-familiar streets of the Island now seemed alien, each step echoing the hollow resonance of his impending exile. The Lion, his dual-bonded familiar, walked alongside him, its majestic form a silent companion in this harrowing journey.

The Island, once a sanctuary suspended above the desolate world, now felt like a prison from which he was being forcibly expelled. The bond with the Lion, now revealed as both a guardian and an omen, intensified the tumult within Tiriaq's heart. The creature's eyes, golden orbs reflecting the turmoil within, locked onto Tiriaq's gaze as if sharing in the burden of their intertwined destinies.

The residents, once his neighbors and friends, cast furtive glances in his direction as he passed. Whispers trailed behind him like lingering shadows, the weight of judgment palpable. The community, so tightly knit before the revelation of his Shadow familiar, now unraveled like a fragile tapestry caught in an unrelenting breeze.

His family, bound by blood but now severed from the embrace of the Island's community, awaited him with a mixture of concern and sorrow. His mother's eyes, once pools of unwavering support, were now clouded with the pain of a mother forced to watch her child face an uncertain fate. His father, a pillar of strength now shaken to its core, offered a solemn nod, the unspoken understanding passing between them like a current of shared grief.

Chapter 3: The Weight of Expectations

In the lofty corridors of the Island, where the weight of expectation hung as palpable as the mist veiling their floating sanctuary, Ayuka moved with the grace expected of the Leader's daughter. The Island, suspended above the desolate world, had embraced tranquility for generations, and as the heir to the leadership, the mantle of responsibility rested heavily on her shoulders. The air was thick with the echoes of whispered hopes and the unspoken aspirations of a community that looked to her with a blend of reverence and anticipation. Each step Ayuka took reverberated with the legacy of her lineage, and the corridors, witnesses to the ebb and flow of Island life, now bore witness to the unfolding destiny of the Leader's daughter.

The Ceremony of Bonds, a revered rite of passage for every resident, unfolded as a nexus of hope and apprehension. As the Leader's daughter, Ayuka found herself at the center of attention, with the eyes of the community tracing her every move. The whispers of anticipation grew louder as the ceremony approached, creating a symphony of expectations that hung like an unspoken melody. Tradition, a guiding force etched into the Island's history, dictated that the Golden familiar, a symbol of leadership and the protector of the Island, would bond with the Leader's kin. However, for Ayuka, the pressure to uphold this time-honored tradition and embody the weighty expectations placed upon her became a burden she carried with grace and trepidation.

On the eve of the ceremony, Ayuka ventured into the labyrinthine caves beneath the Island—a sacred space where she could escape the community's watchful eyes. The crystals lining the cavern walls shimmered with an otherworldly glow, casting dancing reflections on the path ahead.

As the Leader's daughter, Ayuka had explored these caves since childhood, seeking solace amidst the mesmerizing play of light. This time, however, the weight of her impending responsibility mingled with the anticipation of discovering her familiar. Each step felt like a journey into the unknown, a path that would define not just her destiny but the fate of the Island itself. The familiarity of the cave, once a refuge from the demands of her position, now became a crucible where her resolve would be tested, and the echoes of tradition would reverberate in the shadows.

In the heart of the cavern, where the ambient magic hummed like an ancient melody, Ayuka felt a pull—an unseen force guiding her toward her destined companion. Anxiety and excitement coursed through her veins as she approached a figure in the shadows, a majestic Lion exuding an aura of regal brilliance.

As the elders commenced their chant, the air crackled with magic, and the cavern transformed into a kaleidoscope of hues. The crystals responded to the Island's energy, illuminating the space with a radiant glow. Ayuka's heart, however, raced with uncertainty. Would the Golden familiar choose her as its companion, sealing her fate as the Island's next leader? The weight of tradition and the expectations placed upon her as the Leader's daughter intensified with each heartbeat, echoing through the cavern like a drum heralding the unfolding of a momentous destiny.

As the ritual's crescendo enveloped them, the Lion stepped forward, its silhouette now bathed in an ethereal golden light. The realization struck Ayuka with a mixture of awe and trepidation. The Golden familiar, the embodiment of leadership and the Island's protector had chosen her. The weight of expectation, the legacy of her lineage, now manifested in the form of this majestic creature.

In that moment of revelation, a paradox unfolded within Ayuka. Pride swelled at being chosen as the Leader's successor, yet anxiety gnawed at the edges of her confidence. With its radiant presence, the Golden familiar carried the promise of power and the burden of responsibility. Would she be worthy of this honor, or would the shadows that clung to the edges of her thoughts betray the expectations laid upon her? The cavern, once a sanctuary, now echoed the intricacies of Ayuka's internal struggle as she grappled with the magnitude of the destiny that awaited her.

As the residents dispersed, a buzz of excitement filled the cavern. Ayuka, the Leader's daughter, had bonded with the Golden familiar. Yet, beneath the veneer of celebration, the weight of the role she now bore pressed upon her. The Island looked to her for protection, guidance, and a continuation of the legacy that had sustained their peaceful existence.

The echoes of her footsteps reverberated in the cavern as Ayuka walked out into the daylight, the brilliance of the Island above unfolding before her. The celebration continued, but the duality of her emotions consumed her thoughts—a blend of pride and anxiety, a recognition of the expectations and responsibilities now intricately woven into the fabric of her being. The golden glow surrounding her, symbolic of leadership, cast shadows that hinted at the challenges and uncertainties ahead.

As the Leader's daughter, Ayuka's side illuminated the path ahead with the golden glow of the familiar. Yet, the shadows of uncertainty lurked in the recesses of her thoughts. The Ceremony of Bonds, a dance between destiny and doubt, marked not just the beginning of her journey but the commencement of a delicate balance between the radiance of leadership and the veiled truths that awaited in the corridors of the unknown.

The cavern, once a haven of solitude and discovery, now bore witness to Ayuka's internal dialogue as she navigated the transition from heir to leader. The echoes of the ceremonial chant lingered in the air, a constant reminder of the ancient forces that had guided their community for generations. Each step she took, bathed in the golden aura of the familiar, resonated with the weight of tradition and the uncharted territories of leadership. The Island, suspended above the world's desolation, looked to Ayuka to navigate the delicate dance between the brilliance of her golden destiny and the shadows that hinted at the challenges yet to unfold.

Chapter 4: Preparations

As Tiriaq stood at the threshold of departure, the community, sensing the weight of responsibility resting upon his shoulders, rallied with a collective determination to prepare him for the formidable journey into the surface world. Elders, their faces etched with the lines of experience and the tales of yesteryears, surrounded him like pillars of guidance. Each elder brought forth a reservoir of wisdom nurtured by countless seasons, their eyes reflecting the passage of time and the resilience cultivated through adversity.

The elders' gathering was more than a mere farewell; it was a ceremony of wisdom bequeathed from one generation to the next. Their voices, a melodic blend of timeworn tales and practical insights, wove a tapestry that transcended the immediate moment. With each word, they sought to imbue Tiriaq with the essence of their collective knowledge, a legacy that spanned epochs and held the keys to survival in uncharted territories.

The advice offered was about navigating physical landscapes and understanding the intricacies of the human spirit. Elders spoke of the importance of resilience in the face of adversity, the necessity of fostering bonds with unfamiliar faces, and the significance of maintaining a connection to one's roots even when far from home. Like a guardian of tradition, each elder bestowed upon Tiriaq a fragment of the cultural inheritance that had shaped the identity of the floating sanctuary.

As the elders spoke, their words resonated with the practicality of survival and a profound sense of community. The tapestry they wove was a living testament to past, present, and future interconnectedness—an intricate web of experiences and insights meant to fortify Tiriaq for the challenges beyond the floating sanctuary.

Experienced travelers, whose faces bore the weathered imprints of countless encounters and hardships, approached Tiriaq with camaraderie born from shared exploration. Each one carried not just the tangible tools of their trade but also the intangible wealth of experiences gained through navigating the complexities of the surface world. As they spoke, their voices resonated with the echoes of distant landscapes, recounting tales that spanned from the towering peaks to the mysterious depths of uncharted territories.

In this collaborative effort to equip Tiriaq for the unknown, the seasoned travelers extended more than just well-worn advice; they presented tangible tools that would prove indispensable in the unfamiliar landscapes awaiting him. Maps unfolded with a deliberate reverence, revealing the intricate knowledge of those who had traversed these realms before. These maps, marked with the scars of countless explorations, could guide Tiriaq through the vast unknown, pointing out landmarks, cautionary tales, and potential allies.

Survival training, an integral part of Tiriaq's preparation, transcended the theoretical realm and delved into the practical skills honed through generations. The travelers, embodying a living legacy of adaptability, passed down these skills as a crucial arsenal meant to equip Tiriaq with the ability to navigate the unpredictable terrains and unforeseen challenges of the surface world. From identifying edible plants to reading the subtle cues of nature, Tiriaq underwent immersive training that extended beyond the physical tools and into the essence of survival.

In the exchange between the experienced travelers and Tiriaq, a silent understanding existed—recognizing the shared experiences that bound them together as a community. As the travelers imparted their insights, they became both mentors and custodians of the collective knowledge that had allowed the community to thrive in the face of the unknown.

In this collective effort, the community sought to fortify Tiriaq with more than just physical tools. As the elders and seasoned travelers poured their knowledge into

Tiriaq's eager heart, they understood that the journey to the surface world was not merely about survival skills but also about emotional resilience. Stories of resilience became a crucial component, woven into the fabric of his preparation like threads of inspiration. They recounted tales of overcoming challenges, facing the unknown with unwavering determination, and emerging physically unscathed and emotionally intact.

The seasoned travelers, with their faces etched by the experiences of a thousand landscapes, spoke of the importance of adaptability. This quality extended beyond the practicalities of survival and delved into emotional intelligence. They emphasized the significance of maintaining a calm spirit, a resilient heart, and a mind unclouded by anger or resentment. In doing so, Tiriaq realized that his journey was not just a physical expedition but also an emotional odyssey—a quest to discover the surface world and the depths of his character.

As these collective teachings unfolded, a sense of unity and purpose enveloped the community, binding them in a shared commitment to ensure Tiriaq's preparedness for the expedition into the unknown. The unspoken understanding was that his emotional resilience would play a crucial role in the success of his mission, especially in avoiding the pitfalls of anger or bitterness that could cloud his judgment during the inevitable challenges ahead. The collective hope was that Tiriaq would leave not only physically unharmed but also with a heart that remained untarnished by the hardships of exile.

Tiriaq's mother, her eyes reflecting both pride and concern, took him aside, seeking a moment of solitude amid the communal preparations. She began unraveling his heritage's intricate tapestry in the quiet corner of their dwelling. Her words wove through the air like a delicate melody, carrying the echoes of stories that had traversed generations. Each tale, a thread connecting Tiriaq to a legacy hidden beneath the mystique of the Island, resonated with a significance that extended beyond the floating sanctuary.

With a voice of emotion, his mother spoke of Naji, an old family friend who held the keys to unraveling the mysteries of Tiriaq's origin. She explained that Naji was a repository of knowledge, a guardian of secrets, and someone who had shared the joys and sorrows of their family's past. The East, she emphasized, held the key to unlocking the secrets that bound Tiriaq's lineage to the surface world.

As her words unfolded, Tiriaq felt a profound connection to the past, a heritage obscured by the enchantment of the Island. His mother's narrative painted a vivid picture of family ties that transcended the floating sanctuary, reaching into the unknown realm. The significance of heading East now carried a weight that stretched beyond the boundaries of geographical orientation—it became a pilgrimage into the heart of ancestral wisdom and a journey to uncover the truths that lay dormant in the sands of time.

Amid the communal buzz of preparations, this intimate exchange with his mother became pivotal, anchoring Tiriaq to a legacy that beckoned him toward the East. Naji, the old family friend, emerged as a guiding star in the constellation of his unfolding destiny—a connection to the surface world, a bridge between the Island's secrets and the revelations awaiting him beyond its ethereal confines.

As Ayuka delved deeper into the tomes and scrolls that chronicled the Island's history, she found herself immersed in a world where the stories of the past intertwined with the destinies of the present. The leather-bound volumes, aged and weathered, held the collective wisdom of generations, each page revealing fragments of a narrative that danced on the edge of the mystical and the tangible.

With every page turned, Ayuka's quest intensified. Her eyes scanned the archaic texts for clues that could unravel the mystery of the Elders' unwavering belief in exile as the only solution. The answers she sought lay hidden in the cryptic language of prophecies and the accounts of Shadows long forgotten. As her fingertips traversed the timeworn surfaces of the documents, she yearned to understand the precise reasons that compelled the Elders to endorse such a drastic measure.

The flickering candlelight cast shadows that seemed to dance along with the ebb and flow of Ayuka's thoughts. The weight of responsibility hung heavy in the air as she pieced together the fragments of history, seeking to discern patterns and connections that might shed light on the Elders' conviction. The challenge before her was not just to unravel the enigma of previous Shadows but to comprehend the deeper intricacies of the Island's fate and the delicate balance it sought to maintain.

Within the hallowed halls, where the air carried the intoxicating fragrance of aged parchment, Ayuka found solace in her relentless pursuit of knowledge. The soft glow of ancient candles played upon the timeworn shelves and dusty tomes, creating an ambiance that echoed the elusive nature of the information she sought. Each fluttering page beneath her fingers whispered secrets of the past, tales of triumphs and tribulations etched into the very fabric of the Island.

As Ayuka meticulously combed through the annals of time, the flickering candlelight cast dancing shadows on the walls, mirroring the intricate dance of history unfolding before her. The weight of her research became palpable, reflecting the profound gravity of the shadows that now draped a veil of uncertainty over the community. The air seemed charged with the echoes of bygone eras, and Ayuka felt the weight of responsibility intensify with every revelation uncovered within the fragile pages of ancient scrolls.

In this sanctuary of knowledge, where time seemed to stand still, Ayuka delved deeper into the enigmatic narratives that held the key to the Island's past. Pursuing clarity transformed the library into a realm of discovery, where each piece of information added another layer to the intricate tapestry of the Island's history. As shadows played upon the walls, Ayuka sought to unveil not only the mysteries of the Shadows but also the reasons behind the Elders' unwavering conviction in the necessity of exile.

Ayuka's sense of duty, coupled with a fervent desire to safeguard the Island's future, elevated her pursuit of knowledge into a noble quest for clarity. With each deliberate turn of a page and every meticulously deciphered script, she propelled herself closer to unraveling the mysteries delicately veiled in the Island's past. The journey she had undertaken transcended the boundaries of mere intellectual exploration; it was a profound excavation into the foundations that held the essence of the Island's existence.

Her relentless journey through the ancient texts was a meticulous unraveling of threads that wove the narrative of the Island's history. Each revelation, whether etched in ink on crumbling parchment or whispered through the ages, became vital to the puzzle she was determined to solve. Ayuka's quest was not solely about acquiring knowledge; it was a solemn commitment to unearth the secrets that lay buried in the sands of time.

As she delved deeper into the records of eras long gone, Ayuka's pursuit took on a transformative quality. The dusty tomes and time-stained scrolls she sifted through held not just fragments of the past but potential keys to

understanding the challenges that gripped the Island in
the present. In this sacred endeavor, she sought not
only to comprehend the mysteries of the Shadows but
also to grasp the profound significance behind the
Elders' unwavering belief in the necessity of exile.

With every revelation and each uncovered truth, Ayuka
endeavored to illuminate the path forward for the
troubled community. Her tireless dedication echoed
through the hallowed halls of the library, a testament to
the resilience and unwavering spirit of the Leader's
daughter in the face of uncertainty.

Chapter 5: Departure

Amidst the bittersweet farewell, Tiriaq's heart weighed heavy with the complexities of departure. The embrace of his community, once warm and familiar, now held a tinge of sorrow and trepidation. Former friends, whose laughter once echoed through the narrow alleys of the floating Island, exchanged glances that spoke volumes. Elders, guardians of ancient wisdom, conveyed silent acknowledgment, their eyes revealing the shared burden of anticipation for the young adventurer.

As Tiriaq took those first steps away from the congregation, the air seemed charged with unspoken sentiments, suspended between the familiarity of the Island and the uncertainty of the world beyond. The farewell was not just a rite of passage; it was a collective exhalation, a release of hopes and concerns that lingered like mist in the minds of those left behind.

His belongings, carefully packed for the journey, were a tangible link to the life he was leaving behind. The shadowy silhouette of the Lion familiar, a source of both mystery and comfort, paced beside him. Amid the emotional currents, the presence of the enigmatic companion offered a slight solace—an unspoken connection to the Island he called home.

With its majestic floatation and ethereal glow, the Island gradually faded into the distant horizon. As Tiriaq ventured further into the unknown, the gravity of the decision to leave, made palpable by the farewells, settled upon his shoulders. The shadows of doubt and anticipation clung to him like echoes of the mysteries he sought to unravel. With every step, the embrace of the Island waned, replaced by the vast expanse of the surface world, shrouded in both the brilliance of daylight and the veiled secrets of the impending journey.

The descent through the layers of mist marked the stark transition from the ethereal glow of the Island to the harsh reality of the surface. As Tiriaq emerged into the unfiltered sunlight, its intensity pierced through the protective veil of the Island. Blinking against the brilliance, he found himself standing on solid ground, a stark departure from the accustomed sensation of weightless floating.

The landscape stretched before him, an endless panorama of desolation that seemed to defy the vibrant memories of the floating sanctuary. The thin, dry air lacked the comforting touch of the Island's magic. With each breath, Tiriaq felt the absence of the familiar energies that once surrounded him.

His belongings, the meager possessions carefully chosen for the journey, clung to him like echoes of the Island's embrace. The Shadow Lion, his constant companion, walked with regal grace beside him. Against the barren backdrop of the surface world, the shadowy silhouette of the familiar served as a reminder of the connection between the two realms.

Hesitant steps marked Tiriaq's adjustment to the pull of gravity, a force previously alien to the floating sanctuary. The surface world, unforgiving in its vastness, held both the allure of discovery and the daunting challenge of the unknown. As he navigated the unfamiliar terrain, the Shadow Lion moved with a quiet assurance, a silent companion in this uncharted journey beyond the confines of the Island.

The first formidable challenge emerged in the expansive form of the desert—a boundless sea of shifting sands that extended as far as the eye could discern. The unrelenting heat, a relentless force, bore down on Tiriaq as he ventured deeper into the arid expanse. Each step became a dance with mirages, teasing illusions that played tricks on his weary mind.

The grains of sand, carried by the whims of the ever-present wind, formed undulating dunes that stretched like waves frozen in time. The landscape, painted in hues of gold and ochre, seemed to ripple and shimmer under the intense sunlight. The air wavered with the heat, distorting the perception of distance and direction.

Navigating the vastness of the desert became an exercise in resilience for Tiriaq. The Shadow Lion, ever watchful, moved alongside him as a steadfast companion. The shifting sands presented an ever-changing terrain, and the mirages led him on a tantalizing chase, each elusive oasis dissolving into a cruel mirage as he approached.

The relentless sun, unyielding in its gaze, cast elongated shadows that played tricks on Tiriaq's senses. As he pressed forward, the heat-induced mirages continued their dance, a surreal spectacle that tested his determination and ability to discern reality from illusion. Amid this arduous journey, the Shadow Lion's presence offered a silent reassurance, a constant amidst the shifting sands of uncertainty.

In the distance, a group of nomads emerged—a hardy people accustomed to the harsh realities of the desert. Tiriaq approached them, the Shadow Lion at his side, seeking guidance and perhaps a glimpse into the world beyond the Island. Their eyes, weathered by the sun and winds, held a depth of knowledge accumulated through generations.

Initially wary of the newcomer, the nomads soon recognized the unique attire and the determination etched on Tiriaq's face. Through a language of gestures and shared glances, they imparted crucial survival skills, teaching him to navigate the shifting sands and conserve the precious water that sustained life in the unforgiving terrain.

As the nomads shared their insights, caution crept into their exchanges. Through gestures mimicking warriors brandishing weapons, they conveyed the presence of formidable tribes that roamed the vast desert. The nomads' eyes, tinged with a blend of respect and concern, suggested the perils that lay ahead. They spoke of warrior tribes with a reputation for territorial aggression and the need for vigilance in unfamiliar territories. The nomads' warnings echoed like a haunting melody, underscoring the challenges Tiriaq would face beyond the safety of the Island.

Tiriaq's journey, now accompanied by the nomads' wisdom, unfolded as a tapestry woven with challenge and discovery. The desert became a formidable teacher, with its relentless sunsets casting a fiery glow across the horizon and the vast emptiness stretching as far as the eye could see. As he delved deeper into the heart of the arid landscape, the shadows of the Island's mysteries intertwined with the stark realities of the surface world, setting the stage for the revelations that awaited him.

The nomads' guidance became his compass in navigating the shifting sands and unpredictable terrain. Tiriaq, with the Shadow Lion by his side, learned the subtle art of reading the desert's signs—the telltale traces of wind patterns, the shifting dunes that concealed hidden challenges, and the dance of shadows that heralded the changing of the desert's moods.

Each step etched a story into the canvas of Tiriaq's journey, a story of resilience, adaptation, and unraveling the unknown. The nomads' tales of the warrior tribes now echoed in his solitude, adding a layer of caution to the profound beauty of the desert landscape. As the days turned into nights and the sun continued its relentless journey across the sky, Tiriaq's understanding of the world beyond the Island deepened, becoming an intricate mosaic of survival and self-discovery.

Chapter 6: Ayuka's Resolve

In the quiet that lingered after Tiriaq's journey began, Ayuka teetered on the edge of a pivotal decision, one imbued with the power to chart a new course for her life and, by extension, the destiny of the entire Island. Once alive with the hum of scholarly debate and the soft, purposeful strides of knowledge seekers, the corridors and chambers now embraced silence as deep and vast as the oceans cradling their floating sanctuary. This silence was not merely the absence of noise but a dense, expectant waiting, as though the Island's very stones held their breath, anticipating her choice.

Following the advent of the Shadows, Ayuka's life underwent a profound transformation. The balance between her responsibilities as the Leader's daughter and her passion for scholarly inquiry shifted dramatically. Now, she devoted every waking moment to unraveling the mystery of the Shadows. Illuminated by the ambient glow of phosphorescent crystals, she would immerse herself in the ancient texts within the library's sanctum, her fingers gliding over time-worn scripts, her gaze absorbing tales of epochs past when the Island had braved similar darknesses. Despite her diligence, the answers that Ayuka sought—the origins of the Shadows, their essence, and the key to their dissolution—remained elusive, always just out of reach.

The deeper Ayuka delved, the more she became aware
of the glaring omissions in the historical record. It was
as if pieces of a critical puzzle had been deliberately
removed, leaving only cryptic references and half-told
tales of the Island's past dealings with the surface of
ancient times shrouded in shadow and turmoil. Yet, no
document provided a lucid account of how these
perilous times were navigated or the fates of those who
dared to confront the darkness head-on.

The epiphany that the compendium of the Island's lore
might be incomplete—that the answers she yearned for
could lie in the realm from which the Shadows seemed
to emerge—struck Ayuka with a mix of dread and
anticipation. Embarking on a quest beyond the confines
of the Island meant venturing into a world of unknowns,
facing perils unimagined.

Surrounded by the vast repositories of knowledge her
ancestors had amassed, Ayuka felt the acute pang of
their limitations. She recognized that the Island was but
a speck in the grand tapestry of the world, a world that
concealed the truths she sought. This understanding
ignited a fire within her, a determination fueled by the
emergence of the Shadows.

As the threat of the Shadows loomed more prominent
with each passing day, Ayuka's resolve to act
intensified. The Shadows represented not merely a

disturbance to their way of life but a cataclysm that threatened to undo the very essence of their existence. Convinced that the answers lay beyond the Island's serene shores, Ayuka embraced the daunting prospect of seeking them out—not solely for her enlightenment but for the survival and prosperity of all who dwelled upon the Island. Amidst the uncertainty of the path she contemplated, Ayuka's resolve was unwavering, propelled by a compulsion to uncover the truth and a fervent hope that such discoveries might arm her people against the growing tide of darkness.

Her decision to embark on this journey was not just a personal endeavor but a mission carried out under the weight of collective expectations and the silent vigil of the Golden Lion, a symbol of courage and guardianship for her people. It was a testament to her bravery and commitment to securing a brighter, shadow-free future for her Island.

The realization that the secrets she pursued could exist beyond the Island's tranquil shores struck Ayuka with the force of revelation, illuminating her understanding as the dawn scatters the night's deepest shadows. She recognized that the extensive chronicles of the Island's past, for all their depth, harbored voids vast enough to let crucial truths escape unnoticed. The surface world, previously conceived as a distant realm bordering on the mythical, suddenly appeared as a palpable reservoir of knowledge, potentially holding the keys to the enigmas she sought to unlock.

This insight heralded a pivotal moment in Ayuka's path. The prospect that the solution to the Shadows' mystery—and the survival of her people—might be found in the uncharted expanse of the world above filled her with a mixture of trepidation and exhilaration. It nudged her toward a decision that would not only stretch the boundaries of her bravery but also redefine her role as the Leader's daughter and custodian of the Island's heritage.

Choosing to depart from the Island emerged from a deep-seated sense of duty towards her community, a community traditionally inward-looking for insights and direction. The enigmatic nature of the Shadows and their ominous threat demanded a courageous leap into the unknown. Ayuka embraced this daunting venture as her destiny, motivated by a profound commitment to protect her homeland and its denizens.

Her innate curiosity about the Island's past dealings with the surface world further stoked this resolve. What reasons underpinned their prolonged isolation? Which truths had been obscured or lost in the annals of history? The possibility that the answers might not only elucidate the Shadows' essence but also pave the way for a harmonious existence with the surface world lent an additional layer of urgency to her quest.

Fueled by a confluence of duty, curiosity, and a nascent hope that her journey might herald a new epoch for the Island, Ayuka set her sights on a quest replete with unknowns. She was convinced that embracing the courage to explore the unfamiliar and step beyond the sanctuary and security of home constituted the initial stride towards unveiling the truth. This conviction, fortified by the silent accompaniment of the Golden Lion—a quiet sentinel embodying the courage and guardianship revered by her people—guided her decision to forsake the familiar confines of her world in pursuit of revelations that could reshape the destinies of both her people and the estranged worlds they sought to reconnect.

Ayuka's resolve to undertake this quest reflected her deep commitment to her community and her unwavering spirit of perseverance. The prospect of delving into the vast, uncharted realms beyond the Island's tranquil haven presented a formidable challenge. Transitioning from the comforting sounds of the Island's vibrant life to the profound silence that marked her departure underscored the gravity of her journey. At the edge of a significant leap into the unknown, Ayuka stood enveloped in contemplation and fortified by determination.

The morning's early light cast elongated shadows, heralding the journey before her—a journey shrouded in uncertainties yet brimming with the promise of enlightenment. Ayuka was keenly aware that the secrets she sought held the power to transform the future of her homeland. Perhaps, hidden within the annals of the surface world, lay untold stories of ancient encounters with the Shadows or even the keys to understanding their essence and motive. The hope of unearthing such knowledge was the beacon that guided her resolve.

In preparation for her departure, Ayuka had meticulously assembled essential supplies and navigational instruments and imbued herself with the ancestral wisdom encapsulated within selected scrolls. These scrolls, bearing ancient knowledge and maps, connected her people's secluded existence to the expansive realms beneath their aerial sanctuary. They were a poignant reminder of the heritage she sought to preserve and defend.

As the dawn's first rays began to unveil the hidden contours of the world below, Ayuka stood at the threshold between the familiar and the unknown, finding a moment of tranquility amidst the tumult of her emotions. The decision to embark on this path, laden with risks and uncertainties, was nevertheless underscored by a deep-seated sense of purpose.

With a heart full of resolve, she took her first steps toward the unknown, her descent marking the transition from the world she knew to a realm of endless possibilities. The cool air caressed her as she moved further from the Island, each step a testament to her faith in her quest, the convictions that fueled her journey, and the hope that the answers she sought lay just beyond the horizon.

Silently accompanying her was the Golden Lion, her constant companion, and protector. Its presence was a comforting reminder of the strength and courage that lay within her. This journey was not marked by grand gestures or loud declarations but by a quiet resolve that resonated with the core of her being. Ayuka carried with her the collective aspirations of her people, embarking on a quest not solely for knowledge but for the very survival of her community. With every step forward, she edged closer to unraveling the mysteries that threatened her Island's existence, her path illuminated by the unwavering spirit of the Golden Lion by her side.

In Ayuka's heart, a tempest of emotions swirled—a blend of trepidation for the uncharted territories ahead and exhilaration at the prospect of unraveling the enigmas veiled by the surface world. This internal conflict mirrored the intricate tapestry of her roles: as a leader entrusted with her people's well-being and as an intrepid seeker of the unknown. The weight of her community's expectations bore down upon her, their hopeful gazes casting a mantle of responsibility upon her shoulders. They looked to her journey as a glimmer of hope amidst the encroaching shadows.

Yet, amidst the burden of these expectations, Ayuka harbored a flicker of excitement—an eagerness to transcend the confines of her studies and maps, to immerse herself in the diverse tapestry of cultures awaiting her exploration. The prospect of encountering new lands, encountering cultures vastly different from her own, and forging alliances with potential allies brimmed her with anticipation.

As the horizon painted with the hues of dawn heralded the commencement of her descent, Ayuka stood poised at the precipice of the known, her heart aflutter with anticipation. The air pulsated with the promise of a new day, symbolizing the dawn of fresh beginnings. Inhaling the crisp morning air, she steeled herself for the odyssey ahead. The familiarity of the Island, with its ethereal beauty and protective embrace, faded into the background as she ventured into the boundless unknown.

Though fraught with perils and uncertainties, her journey also held the promise of revelations that could reshape the destiny of her homeland and its inhabitants. The path ahead, shrouded in veils of uncertainty, beckoned her onward, propelled by an unwavering conviction in the imperative of her quest. Ayuka harbored the belief that the answers she sought lay concealed somewhere amidst the vast expanse below, awaiting discovery beneath layers of time and distance.

With each stride away from the Island, Ayuka delved deeper into a realm poised to challenge her in unprecedented ways. Yet, it was precisely this crucible of challenges, this voyage into the heart of the unknown, that sparked a flame of hope within her. Hope that her endeavors would not only unravel the mysteries of the Shadows but also forge a path toward a future where her people could thrive, liberated from the specter that had driven her from her homeland. Despite the uncertainties ahead, Ayuka's spirit remained resolute, driven by the conviction that the salvation of her home hinged upon the truths she sought to unearth.

Chapter 7: A Warrior Tribe

The relentless sun hung high in the cloudless sky, its rays scorching the barren landscape with an intensity that seemed to defy the very essence of life. Tiriaq trudged onward through the endless expanse of sand, each step sending cascades of fine grains swirling into the air. The horizon stretched before him like an unending mirage, teasing with the promise of relief that never materialized.

With every passing moment, the oppressive heat bore down upon him, sapping his strength and resolve. Beads of sweat formed on his brow, evaporating almost instantly in the searing heat. The shifting sands beneath his feet seemed to conspire against him, pulling at his limbs with an invisible force that threatened to drag him down into the depths of the desert.

As Tiriaq pressed forward, the shadows cast by the midday sun stretched out across the landscape like dark tendrils, weaving a tapestry of deception that obscured the true nature of his surroundings. The distant dunes shimmered in the heat haze, their contours shifting and warping with each passing moment, leaving him disoriented and uncertain of his path.

Yet, despite the overwhelming odds stacked against him, Tiriaq forged onward, driven by a determination that burned bright within him. With each step, he pushed himself to the limits of his endurance, his resolve unyielding in the face of adversity. He knew that only by pressing forward, by confronting the harsh realities of the desert head-on, could he hope to uncover the answers he sought and emerge victorious against the shadows that threatened to engulf him.

As the day wore on and the relentless sun beat down upon him, Tiriaq's keen senses detected a subtle shift in the air—a faint disturbance on the horizon that hinted at the presence of others in this desolate expanse. Squinting against the glare, he saw the telltale movement of figures emerging from the shifting sands, their forms distorted by the heat haze that danced upon the dunes.

A group of warriors, their silhouettes wavering in the shimmering heat, advanced towards Tiriaq with purposeful strides. Each step kicked up clouds of sand, swirling around them like a cloak of dust, while their weapons glinted menacingly in the harsh sunlight. They wielded an array of weaponry—gleaming scimitars, wickedly curved daggers, and sturdy shields adorned with intricate designs that spoke of battles won and lives lost.

Their eyes shadowed beneath the brims of weathered turbans, bore the steely gaze of those who had faced countless trials in this unforgiving land. There was a primal intensity to their movements, a sense of predatory instinct honed by years of survival amidst the harsh realities of the desert. As they drew closer, Tiriaq could feel the weight of their intent bearing down upon him, a silent challenge that demanded his attention.

With his heart pounding in his chest, Tiriaq's hands tightened around the weapon he had hastily grabbed from home, an old dagger—a feeble attempt at defense against the encroaching threat. His mind raced, searching desperately for a way out as the warriors closed in, their ominous presence casting a shadow over the barren landscape.

Tiriaq's fear threatened to overwhelm him with each step they took, but a stubborn determination ignited within him. He knew he had to stand his ground to face this danger head-on, even if his chances of survival seemed slim. So, with trembling hands and a resolve born of necessity, he raised his makeshift weapon in a vain but courageous attempt to defend himself against the looming onslaught.

As despair threatened to consume him, a sudden shift in the wind caught Tiriaq's attention. The sand danced and swirled around him as if stirred by some unseen force. Then, from the midst of the swirling sands, a low, ominous growl pierced the air, sending shivers down Tiriaq's spine.

Turning toward the source of the sound, Tiriaq's eyes widened in awe and disbelief as he beheld the form of a majestic lion emerging from the shadows—a creature bathed in a radiant golden light that seemed to defy the harshness of the desert. Its eyes gleamed with an otherworldly brilliance, and its presence exuded an aura of power and protection.

For a fleeting moment, Tiriaq felt a surge of hope wash over him, his fear momentarily forgotten in the presence of this magnificent beast. But as quickly as it had appeared, the golden lion vanished into the swirling sands, leaving Tiriaq to wonder if it had been a figment of his imagination or a miraculous intervention from a higher power.

In that moment of peril, Tiriaq felt a surge of courage coursing through his veins. With the enigmatic Shadow Lion by his side, he was infused with a newfound sense of strength and determination. Despite the overwhelming odds stacked against him, he stood his ground, drawing upon his Shadowy companion's silent guidance and unwavering presence.

As the warriors advanced, their weapons gleaming menacingly in the harsh desert sunlight, Tiriaq felt a calm resolve settling over him. With a swift and decisive motion, he raised his weapon, his grip steady and unwavering. Beside him, the Shadow Lion radiated an aura of fierce determination, its form shimmering with an ethereal light that seemed to dance with the heat of the desert.

The Shadow Lion leaped into action in a blur of motion, moving with a grace and agility that defied its size. With a mighty roar reverberating through the desert landscape, it launched at the approaching warriors, claws baring and teeth gleaming. The sheer force of its presence sent the warriors staggering backward, their ranks thrown into disarray by the unexpected onslaught.

Tiriaq watched in awe as the Shadow Lion fought with a ferocity that bordered on the supernatural. Its movements were fluid and precise, effortlessly dispatching each opponent that dared challenge it. With each strike, Tiriaq felt a surge of admiration and gratitude toward his newfound companion, whose silent guidance and unwavering support had proven his salvation in imminent danger.

With the immediate threat dispelled and a newfound sense of safety settling over him, Tiriaq turned to the

Shadow Lion, his heart filled with gratitude and curiosity. In the depths of the creature's luminous gaze, he saw a glimmer of understanding, as if the majestic beast recognized their shared bond and the silent guidance it had offered him in his time of need.

Tiriaq approached the Shadow Lion cautiously, his movements reverent as he reached out a trembling hand to touch the creature's golden fur. To his surprise, the lion lowered its head, allowing Tiriaq to make contact. As their gazes met, Tiriaq felt a sense of connection that transcended words—a silent communication that spoke of trust and mutual respect.

At that moment, Tiriaq realized that the Shadow Lion was not merely a guardian or protector but a companion—a steadfast ally who had chosen to stand by his side in his darkest hour. With a grateful smile, Tiriaq whispered words of thanks to the creature, knowing that their bond would guide him through the challenges that lay ahead on his journey through the unforgiving desert.

Though Tiriaq couldn't shake the feeling that there was more to the Shadow Lion than met the eye, he found solace in the unwavering presence of his enigmatic companion. There was a depth to the creature's gaze, a wisdom that transcended the limitations of speech—a silent understanding that resonated with Tiriaq on a profound level. Despite the mysteries that shrouded the Shadow Lion's true nature, Tiriaq trusted in its guidance, knowing instinctively that their bond would see him through the trials ahead.

With the Shadow Lion by his side, Tiriaq pressed onward into the unknown, his footsteps guided by a newfound sense of purpose. The vast expanse of the desert stretched before them, its secrets hidden beneath the shifting sands and scorching sun. Yet, Tiriaq faced the challenges ahead with courage born of companionship, and his resolve was strengthened by the knowledge that he was not alone in his journey. As they ventured deeper into the heart of the desert, Tiriaq embraced the uncertainty of the path before him, knowing that with the Shadow Lion at his side, he would find the strength to overcome whatever obstacles lay in their way.

Chapter 8: Whispers of the Past

In the quiet of the approaching dusk, Tiriaq's heart quickened with more than just the thrill of discovery. These ancient and silent ruins held the promise of unraveling the threads of his past. His grandfather's stories of a lineage tied to the guardians of balance, to those who once walked alongside the creatures of shadow and light, echoed in his mind. Could there be a connection, however faint, between his family's history and the secrets these crumbling walls held?

Though eroded by time, the symbols carved into the archway sparked a flicker of recognition in Tiriaq. They resembled the intricate patterns etched into the heirlooms passed down through his family—artifacts he had once dismissed as mere trinkets, their significance lost to time. Standing before the remnants of a world long gone, Tiriaq wondered if these pieces were keys to understanding the ancient pact mentioned in the legends.

As he traced the lines of the symbols with his fingers, the Shadow Lion stirred, its gaze fixed on Tiriaq with an intensity that spoke volumes. It was as though the creature recognized the significance of this moment, understanding Tiriaq's desire to bridge the gap between his present and the echoes of his ancestors' whispers.

With each step into the heart of the ruins, Tiriaq felt as though he was walking in the footsteps of those who came before him. The air around him seemed charged with the residue of ancient magic, a testament to the deep connection this place held to the guardians of balance. It was a connection that, perhaps, his family had once shared, a lineage blessed—or burdened—with a role in the great tapestry of this land's history.

The notion that he might find some clue, hinting at his ancestors' involvement with creatures like the Shadow Lion, fueled Tiriaq's determination. Each chamber explored, and each puzzle solved brought him closer to understanding the legacy he inherited, a legacy of guardianship over the balance between light and shadow. In the silence of the ruins, with the Shadow Lion by his side, Tiriaq dared to hope that he would uncover the link that bound his past to the path he now walked.

Tiriaq stepped closer to the archway, his eyes scanning the intricacies of the carvings. Though worn by the elements, the symbols were deeply etched into the stone, suggesting their significance had warranted enduring the passage of time. They were a complex amalgamation of geometric patterns and stylized figures, reminiscent of the tales of guardians and mythical beasts his grandfather used to recount. Among them, the image of a lion, not unlike the Shadow Lion, was prominently featured, its mane depicted as a halo of light, perhaps indicating a revered status.

This motif of the lion reappeared throughout the architecture of the ruins, serving as a leitmotif that guided Tiriaq deeper into the heart of the ancient city. Though now mere skeletons of their former glory, the buildings bore the elegance of a civilization that had once thrived. Pillars stood tall against the test of time, their capitals adorned with carvings of the natural world - trees, rivers, and animals in harmony, suggesting a society that had lived in close communion with the land and its creatures.

The pathways between the structures were lined with statues, many of which had succumbed to the sands, yet those that remained intact depicted figures with an aura of nobility, their gazes fixed on the horizon as if looking towards a future they would never see. Some held staves or wore amulets bearing the same lion symbol, reinforcing the idea of a guardianship role these individuals must have played.

Tiriaq noted the symbols meticulously, sketching them in a small journal he had taken to carrying. He made special note of the recurring lion motif, drawing parallels between the depiction of the lions in the ruins and the appearance of the Shadow Lion. The craftsmanship of the ruins suggested that this civilization possessed advanced knowledge and skills, not only in architecture but also in their understanding of the balance between the spiritual and the material world.

The air within the ruins was thick with the scent of history, each stone symbolizing a piece of a puzzle that spanned millennia. As he moved through the archway, stepping over the threshold into the city proper, Tiriaq couldn't shake the feeling that these ruins were a bridge to the past, one that might hold the key to understanding not only the Shadow Lion's origins but also his family's legacy and the role they played in the ancient tales of guardianship and balance.

In this central chamber, the air felt different, almost charged with an ancient energy that pulsed softly underfoot. Tiriaq's steps echoed as he moved closer to the frescoes, his fingers brushing against the cool stone as if to connect with the spirits of those who had once roamed these halls. The images painted a vivid picture of a society where humans and mystical creatures coexisted, thriving together in a balance that seemed almost utopian. Central to this harmony was the lion, depicted not just as a beast but as a revered entity, a guardian of both realms.

The fresco that captivated Tiriaq the most was an expansive mural that spanned the length of the chamber wall. It depicted a grand procession of humans and creatures, leading towards a radiant figure seated atop a throne - the lion with its mane of golden light. The creatures around it varied in form; some basked in light while others melded with the shadows, yet all looked reverently towards the lion. Notably, the lion's gaze was directed not at its followers but beyond the mural, as if it saw something unseen by the others. Deep and knowing, its eyes bore a striking similarity to the Shadow Lion's gaze, a mix of wisdom and a melancholy understanding of the burdens of its role.

Tiriaq couldn't help but draw parallels between the depicted lion and his companion. The Shadow Lion had always been a figure of protection and guidance, its presence comforting yet mysterious. However, the lion in the mural, with its halo of golden light, suggested a being of physical and immense spiritual power capable of bridging worlds. The differences were palpable, yet the essence seemed the same. Could it be, he pondered, that the Shadow Lion was once revered as the lion in the fresco? Or perhaps they were different manifestations of the same entity, shaped by the beliefs and needs of those it chose to guide.

As Tiriaq absorbed the mural's details, he noticed smaller symbols and inscriptions at the base of the fresco, possibly prayers or accolades directed at the lion. These inscriptions were written in a familiar script, yet beyond his immediate comprehension. He took his time to sketch these as well, hoping they might later unlock further secrets about the connection between the Shadow Lion and the golden lion of the mural.

Turning to the Shadow Lion, Tiriaq sought any sign of recognition or reaction to the depictions before them. The creature sat, its gaze fixed on the mural, an inscrutable sentinel. Yet, in the depths of its eyes, a light flickered that mirrored the lion's radiance in the fresco, a silent testament to a shared legacy that spanned the divide between shadow and light, past and present.

Tiriaq observed the puzzle with a mix of curiosity and trepidation. The mechanism consisted of a large stone panel set into the wall, adorned with glyphs that resembled those etched into the archway entrance and around the frescoes. Beside the panel, a collection of levers carved with different symbols stood in a silent row, like sentinels guarding a secret. The symbols on the levers mirrored those on the panel, suggesting a direct correlation between the two.

The puzzle seemed to be a lock of sorts, one that required a precise combination to unlock further secrets hidden within the ruins. Tiriaq approached, his gaze shifting from the levers to the glyphs and back again, trying to decipher the connection. The glyphs were cryptic, their meanings obscured by time and the esoteric knowledge of a long-gone civilization.

The Shadow Lion's actions caught his attention as he studied the panel. The creature paused at specific glyphs, its tail flicking lightly against them. Tiriaq noted these glyphs carefully—the lion, the sun, and what appeared to be a representation of shadow merging with light. It seemed the Shadow Lion was guiding him, offering silent hints through its behavior.

Taking a deep breath, Tiriaq reached out to the levers, his hands hovering hesitantly. He decided to trust the silent guidance offered by his companion, choosing the levers that corresponded to the glyphs the Shadow Lion had indicated. The lion was symbolic of their shared journey; the sun was a nod to the golden radiance that occasionally shimmered through the Shadow Lion's mane, and the merging shadows and light was perhaps a representation of their very essence.

With each lever pulled, a soft click echoed through the chamber, a sound that grew increasingly satisfying as it indicated his choices were correct—after adjusting the last lever, a moment of silence hung in the air, thick with anticipation. Then, with a rumble that vibrated through the stone floor and into the soles of his feet, a section of the wall slid away, revealing a hidden passage.

The air flowing from the newly opened passage was cooler, carrying a faint hint of moisture and the musty scent of untouched spaces. Tiriaq couldn't help but feel a swell of pride at having solved the puzzle, but he knew, deep down, that the guidance of the Shadow Lion had led to this success. The creature seemed unfazed by their progress, yet its steady gaze on the hidden passage suggested an understanding of the importance of what lay ahead.

Together, they stood at the threshold of deeper secrets, the ruins beckoning them further into its heart. Tiriaq took a moment to glance at the Shadow Lion, acknowledging the creature's role in their discovery. With a newfound sense of partnership and curiosity, they stepped into the passage, ready to face whatever mysteries awaited them in the shadows.

Descending into the passage, Tiriaq and the Shadow Lion entered a realm where the light of the desert sun could not reach. Here, the air was cool and still, as if the very breath of the earth was holding its anticipation of their journey. The passage narrowed, leading them through a labyrinthine network of tunnels that tested Tiriaq's physical agility and mental fortitude. With its innate connection to the shadows, the Shadow Lion navigated these challenges with serene confidence, its glowing eyes cutting through the darkness.

Their first challenge was a corridor lined with pressure plates hidden beneath a thin layer of sand. A misstep triggered a series of sharp spears to shoot from the walls. Tiriaq observed as the Shadow Lion tread carefully, its steps precise and deliberate. Mimicking its movements, he crossed the corridor unscathed, each step a lesson in trust and observation.

Next, they came upon a room with a ceiling supported by pillars, and between them, pits filled with darkness yawned wide. The Shadow Lion leaped from pillar to pillar with graceful ease, its form barely touching the stone before moving on. Tiriaq followed, his heart pounding with each jump. The risk of falling into the unknown below tested his courage, but the steady presence of the Shadow Lion spurred him on, its confidence lending him strength.

The most daunting challenge, however, lay in a vast chamber they discovered, its center occupied by a deep chasm. The only way across was a narrow stone bridge, worn by time and missing sections. The Shadow Lion crossed first, its form almost merging with the shadows as it navigated the treacherous path. Tiriaq took a deep breath, focusing on the bond that had grown between them. Step by cautious step, he crossed the bridge, the abyss below a constant reminder of the peril they faced together.

The bond between Tiriaq and the Shadow Lion with each challenge they overcame deepened. The creature's guidance was more than just physical; it was a source of emotional strength for Tiriaq, a reminder that he was not alone in this dark, ancient place. The shadows that had once seemed menacing now felt like a protective cloak, wrapping around him with the comforting familiarity of the Shadow Lion's presence.

As they moved deeper into the ruins, the challenges they faced tested not just their physical abilities but also their resolve and trust in each other. The Shadow Lion's silent support was a beacon for Tiriaq, guiding him through the darkness and toward the secrets waiting in the ruins' heart. Together, they ventured onward, united in their quest to uncover the mysteries of the past and the connection between Tiriaq's lineage and the enigmatic Shadow Lion that walked beside him.

They found it at the heart of the ruins—a chamber whose center held an orb pulsating with a light that mirrored the hues of the desert sun at dawn. Tiriaq's breath caught in his throat as he beheld the mesmerizing sight, feeling a strange pull towards the radiant orb. Beside him, the Shadow Lion's form seemed to shimmer, its edges blurring as if it were a mirage born of the desert's heat. Yet, its unwavering and intense gaze remained fixed upon Tiriaq, urging him forward with silent insistence.

Drawn by a force he could not fully comprehend, Tiriaq stepped closer to the orb, his heart pounding in anticipation. The air crackled with energy, and a sense of anticipation hung thick in the chamber as if the very stones were holding their collective breath in anticipation of what was to come. The closer Tiriaq approached, the more pronounced the shimmering of the Shadow Lion became until its form seemed to blend seamlessly with the dancing light of the orb.

With each step, Tiriaq felt a surge of emotions welling within him—an amalgamation of awe, curiosity, and a hint of trepidation. What secrets lay hidden within this chamber? What connection did the orb and the Shadow Lion hold to his destiny? As he reached out to touch the orb, his fingertips tingled with anticipation, and a sense of exhilaration washed over him, mingling with the cool, electric energy that filled the air.

As Tiriaq's fingertips brushed against the smooth surface of the orb, a surge of energy coursed through him, and he was enveloped in a swirling vortex of light and shadow. In the depths of his mind, a vision began to unfold—a tapestry of memories and prophecies woven together in a dazzling display.

Amidst the ethereal glow, the figure of the golden lion emerged, its form radiant yet shrouded in the shifting shadows. Its roar echoed through the chamber, a haunting symphony of light and darkness intertwined. With each reverberation, Tiriaq felt the weight of ancient knowledge wash over him, carrying the echoes of a long past.

The lion's voice, a mesmerizing blend of shadow and light, resonated within Tiriaq's soul as it recounted tales of a bygone era—a time when balance reigned supreme and harmony bound the realms together. But as the vision unfolded, Tiriaq saw glimpses of a looming threat, a darkness that crept insidiously from the shadows, threatening to engulf the world in eternal night.

Amid this chaos, the golden lion stood as the guardian of balance, its majestic form embodying light and shadow. It spoke of a forgotten pact between the people and the creatures that walked between worlds—a bond that had once ensured the delicate equilibrium of existence. Yet, with each passing generation, the memory of this ancient alliance faded, and the lion's power waned, leaving the world vulnerable to the encroaching darkness.

As the vision faded, Tiriaq felt a sense of urgency gripping his heart. The golden lion's words echoed in his mind, urging him to heed the call of destiny and reclaim the balance that had been lost. With newfound clarity, Tiriaq understood the significance of his journey and the pivotal role he would play in shaping the world's fate.

As the last echoes of the vision faded, Tiriaq found himself once again standing in the ancient chamber, the soft glow of the orb casting an otherworldly light upon the stone walls. Beside him, the Shadow Lion remained, its presence a steadfast anchor in the wake of the revelations they had witnessed together. Though the connection between the golden lion of the past and his enigmatic companion remained shrouded in mystery, Tiriaq sensed a deeper understanding blossoming within him.

Stepping out of the ruins, Tiriaq emerged into the harsh light of the desert sun, his mind abuzz with newfound knowledge and purpose. The journey through the ancient ruins had irrevocably changed him, revealing layers of strength and resilience he hadn't known he possessed. The challenges he had faced within the ruins had tested his courage and determination, forcing him to confront fears and weaknesses that had long lain dormant within his soul.

Yet, amidst the trials and tribulations, Tiriaq had also discovered a wellspring of inner strength, a resilience forged in the crucible of adversity. With each step he took, the weight of the knowledge he had gained settled upon his shoulders, infusing him with a sense of purpose that burned brighter than ever. Guided by the enigmatic presence of the Shadow Lion, Tiriaq felt a newfound clarity coursing through his veins, illuminating the path ahead with the promise of hope and redemption.

As they ventured into the vast expanse of the desert, Tiriaq knew that their journey was far from over. The secrets of the past had illuminated the path toward an uncertain future. Still, it was a path they would tread together, bound by the unbreakable bond of companionship and shared destiny. With the Shadow Lion at his side, Tiriaq set his sights on the horizon, his heart brimming with determination and resolve. Whatever trials awaited them on the road ahead, he knew they would face them together, united in their quest to safeguard the world from the encroaching darkness.

Chapter 9: A Journey

As Ayuka and the Golden Lion journeyed through diverse landscapes, their path led them across barren deserts, where the relentless sun beat down upon the shimmering sands, to lush oases where life flourished in abundance, and through ancient forests where the trees whispered secrets of ages past. Each environment presented challenges and revelations, testing the duo's resolve and deepening their understanding of the world.

In the barren deserts, Ayuka and the Golden Lion faced the unrelenting challenge of survival in a landscape that seemed determined to test their resilience at every turn. The scorching sun beat down upon them with merciless intensity, its searing rays threatening to drain their strength with each passing hour. They trudged across endless stretches of shifting dunes, their progress slow and arduous as they battled against the relentless force of nature.

Navigating the treacherous terrain, Ayuka and the Golden Lion encountered formidable obstacles at every step. Fierce sandstorms whipped through the desert, their raging winds obscuring their vision and tearing at their clothing with savage fury. Blinded by the swirling sands, they pressed onward, their determination unyielding in the face of adversity.

Yet, amidst the harshness of their surroundings, Ayuka and the Golden Lion discovered hidden oases—mirages of life amidst the desert's desolation. These sanctuaries, concealed from the outside world by veils of shimmering heat, offered a welcome reprieve from the sun's relentless onslaught. With each oasis they stumbled upon, their arrival was met by a chorus of grateful whispers from the parched earth as if the land rejoiced in their presence.

In these fleeting moments of respite, Ayuka and the Golden Lion took the opportunity to replenish their dwindling supplies and rejuvenate their spirits. They drank deeply from the cool, refreshing waters of the oasis, their thirst quenched by the life-giving liquid that flowed from hidden springs beneath the desert sands. They rested beneath the shade of ancient palm trees, their weary bodies finding solace in the embrace of nature's bounty.

Yet, even as they reveled in the oasis's temporary shelter, Ayuka and the Golden Lion knew that their journey was far from over. With each passing day, they ventured deeper into the heart of the desert, their resolve unshaken by the challenges ahead. For amidst the barren wasteland, they knew that there were still mysteries waiting to be uncovered and truths waiting to be revealed. And with the Golden Lion as their guide, they pressed onward, their spirits undaunted by the trials that awaited them.

In the lush oases, Ayuka and the Golden Lion were immersed in a world of vibrant vitality, a stark juxtaposition to the harshness of the surrounding desert. Life flourished in abundance here, manifesting in a tapestry of colors and scents that captivated the senses. They wandered through verdant groves adorned with lush foliage; their footsteps softened by a carpet of emerald-green grasses and delicate wildflowers that danced in the gentle breeze.

The oasis was a sanctuary of serenity, where the air was rich with the sweet fragrance of blossoms and the earthy scent of fertile soil. Ayuka and the Golden Lion marveled at the beauty of cascading waterfalls that tumbled gracefully down rocky cliffs, their crystalline waters shimmering in the dappled sunlight. They followed meandering streams that wound their way through the oasis, their melodies a soothing symphony that harmonized with the rustle of leaves and the chorus of birdsong that filled the air.

Yet, amidst the tranquility of the oasis, Ayuka and the Golden Lion remained vigilant, mindful of the hidden dangers that lurked beneath the surface of this idyllic paradise. Beneath the lush foliage and shimmering waters, they discovered the delicate balance between life and death, growth and decay. They encountered predators that stalked the shadows, their keen senses honed to detect the slightest movement amidst the dense underbrush. They witnessed the relentless cycle of nature, where the beauty of life was intertwined with the inevitability of death—a reminder of the fragility of existence and the impermanence of all things.

Despite the dangers that lurked amidst the verdant beauty of the oasis, Ayuka and the Golden Lion found solace in the sanctuary of nature's embrace. Here, amidst the abundance of life, they discovered a sense of peace—a respite from the trials of their journey and a reminder of the inherent resilience of the natural world. As they continued on their path, their spirits renewed by the rejuvenating power of the oasis, they carried with them the knowledge that even in the harshest of environments, life would always find a way to flourish.

In the heart of the ancient forests, Ayuka and the Golden Lion entered a realm untouched by the passage of time, where towering trees stood as silent sentinels, their gnarled roots intertwining with the earth like ancient storytellers weaving tales of old. The air was thick with the heady scent of earth and moss, and beams of golden sunlight pierced through the dense canopy above, illuminating the forest floor with a celestial glow.

As they ventured deeper into the forest's embrace, Ayuka and the Golden Lion were surrounded by an otherworldly beauty—a landscape of unparalleled majesty and mystery. The trees, their ancient limbs stretching skyward like fingers reaching for the heavens, seemed to pulse with quiet energy, their rustling leaves whispering secrets that only the most attentive could decipher.

Amidst the towering giants, Ayuka and the Golden Lion encountered guardians of the forest—beings as old as time itself, their presence a testament to the enduring spirit of the natural world. These ethereal beings, with eyes that gleamed like orbs of polished amber, regarded Ayuka and the Golden Lion with a mixture of curiosity and caution as if weighing the intentions of these intruders in their sacred domain.

As they moved deeper into the forest's heart, Ayuka and the Golden Lion listened intently to the ancient voices that echoed through the trees, their words laden with wisdom and warning. They heard tales of epochs long past, of civilizations risen and fallen, and of the eternal dance between light and shadow that shaped the destiny of the world. And amidst the symphony of whispers that filled the forest's air, they sensed a profound connection to the land. This bond transcended time and space, linking them to the ancient guardians who watched over its secrets with unyielding vigilance.

In the depths of the ancient forest, Ayuka and the Golden Lion were enveloped in a symphony of whispers, each rustle of leaves and creak of branches carrying the weight of centuries-old tales. The voices of the trees spoke of epochs long past, painting vivid pictures of civilizations risen and fallen, their echoes reverberating through the very fabric of the forest.

Amidst the murmurs of the ancient guardians, Ayuka and the Golden Lion learned of the delicate balance that governed the natural world—a balance between light and shadow, life and death, creation and destruction. They heard of times when the forces of darkness threatened to engulf the land and of the brave souls who stood as guardians, their unwavering resolve keeping the darkness at bay.

Yet, intertwined with tales of struggle and strife were stories of hope and resilience—of beings who dared to defy fate and forge their destinies. Ayuka and the Golden Lion listened with rapt attention, their hearts filled with a profound reverence for the land and its guardians, whose watchful eyes had witnessed the ebb and flow of time itself.

With each whispered tale and a fleeting glimpse of ancient wisdom, Ayuka and the Golden Lion felt their resolve strengthen, their purpose clear. They were not merely travelers passing through the forest—they were guardians, entrusted with the sacred duty of preserving the delicate balance of the world and protecting it from the encroaching forces that threatened to consume it.

And so, with hearts filled with reverence and determination, Ayuka and the Golden Lion pressed onward, their journey through the ancient forest guided by the echoes of the past and the promise of an unwritten future.

Chapter 10: The Strife

Amid their journey, Ayuka and the Golden Lion stumbled upon a conflict that transcended the boundaries of the physical world. Dark forces, cloaked in malevolence and driven by insatiable greed, had unearthed ancient artifacts imbued with dark energy, seeking to bend them to their will and wield unimaginable power.

These malevolent entities, their hearts consumed by the darkness they sought to harness, posed a grave threat not only to Ayuka and the Golden Lion but to the very essence of the natural world. Their twisted desires knew no bounds, and they would stop at nothing to achieve their goals, heedless of the chaos and destruction they left in their wake.

In the heart of the desolate wasteland, where the sinister minions of darkness surrounded, the air crackled with dark energy, Ayuka and the Golden Lion. Eyes aglow with malevolent intent, the creatures emerged from the shadows, their twisted forms contorted by the corrupting influence of the dark energy that permeated the land.

With a primal roar, the leader of the dark forces stepped forward, its presence casting a pall of fear over the barren landscape. Its eyes, twin orbs of darkness, fixated upon Ayuka and the Golden Lion, hungering for the power that pulsed within them.

But Ayuka stood resolute, her gaze unwavering as she met the creature's stare. Beside her, the Golden Lion radiated with an ethereal light, its mane ablaze with golden fire. In that moment, they were not merely two beings confronting a formidable foe—they were embodiments of light and hope in a world threatened by darkness.

Amid the chaos, as Ayuka and the Golden Lion stood back to back, their foes closing in from all sides, Ayuka felt a surge of energy coursing through her veins. With a sudden clarity, she saw a vision of the Shadow Lion—a shimmering silhouette amidst a sea of darkness, its eyes blazing with an otherworldly light.

In that moment of connection, Ayuka felt a profound sense of purpose wash over her. The vision of the Shadow Lion fueled her drive, filling her with an unyielding determination to stand against the forces of darkness and protect the world from their malevolent grasp.

With renewed vigor, Ayuka channeled the ancient energies of the natural world through her staff, unleashing torrents of light and energy that surged forth to meet their adversaries head-on. Beside her, the

Golden Lion roared, its majestic form radiating with a blinding light that banished the shadows and instilled hope in those who fought alongside them.

As they stood amidst the conflict's aftermath, Ayuka couldn't shake the feeling that there was more to the Golden Lion than met the eye. Its radiant presence, unwavering loyalty, and the enigmatic connection she felt with it all hint at a more profound truth waiting to be uncovered.

In moments of quiet reflection, Ayuka pondered the nature of the Golden Lion and its resemblance to the Shadow Lion she had encountered in her visions. The similarities between the two were undeniable—their majestic presence, their ability to harness the forces of light against the encroaching darkness, and the profound sense of guidance they provided in times of need.

Yet, amidst these similarities, there were also subtle differences that set them apart. While the Shadow Lion had appeared to her as a vision, shrouded in mystery and veiled in darkness, the Golden Lion stood before her as a tangible, radiant embodiment of light and hope.

As Ayuka gazed into the Golden Lion's luminous eyes, she couldn't help but wonder if there was more to their connection than she realized. Though the answers eluded her for now, Ayuka couldn't shake the feeling that the truth lay waiting to be discovered, hidden within the depths of the natural world they traversed. With each step forward, she was filled with anticipation, knowing that the journey ahead held the key to unlocking the mysteries of the Golden Lion and its connection to the Shadow Lion. As they ventured into the unknown, Ayuka remained vigilant, ready to uncover the secrets hidden beneath their shared reality.

Chapter 11: A Pilgrimage

As Tiriaq and the Shadow Lion embarked on their journey, the frozen tundras stretched before them like a vast, icy canvas waiting to be explored. The biting winds, more than just a chill in the air, were like skilled sculptors, crafting the ice and snow into eerie shapes that danced along the horizon. Each gust carried a haunting melody, a symphony of winter that echoed through the desolate expanse.

The air seemed to freeze around them, turning their breath into fleeting clouds of crystalline mist. With every step, the ground beneath their feet groaned and shifted, the sound reverberating through the frozen landscape like a warning from the icy depths below. Snowdrifts threatened to engulf them, hiding treacherous crevices that could swallow them whole with a single misstep. And yet, amidst the peril, there was a haunting beauty to be found—a beauty that captivated Tiriaq and the Shadow Lion even as it tested their endurance and resilience.

Emerging from the icy embrace of the tundra, Tiriaq, and the Shadow Lion found themselves immersed in verdant valleys brimming with vitality. These valleys stood in stark juxtaposition to the tundra's desolation, a vibrant tapestry of life woven by nature's nurturing touch. Rivers meandered gracefully through the landscape, their melodious murmurs echoing the land's heartbeat while lush vegetation flourished along their banks.

In this thriving ecosystem, every corner teemed with activity. Insects danced amidst the foliage, their delicate wings shimmering in the dappled sunlight, while birds filled the air with joyful songs. Tiriaq and the Shadow Lion stood in awe of the intricate web of life surrounding them, from the delicate petals of wildflowers to the towering canopy of ancient trees that whispered secrets to the sky.

Together, they wandered through this lush paradise, their senses alive with the sights and sounds of nature's bounty. Each step brought them closer to understanding the delicate balance that sustained this thriving ecosystem. As they journeyed deeper into the valley, they felt a profound sense of connection to the land and all its inhabitants. All the while, their goal remained on their minds.

Their journey led them deep into the bowels of ancient caverns, where the very essence of the earth seemed to pulse through the stones. These caverns stood as silent witnesses to the passage of time, their vast chambers echoing with the whispers of ancient secrets. High above, the ceilings vanished into the darkness while the ground stretched into abyssal depths below.

The air within these caverns was heavy with the scent of minerals and damp earth, suffusing every breath with a sense of ancient wisdom. With each step, their footfalls reverberated against the cavern walls, a testament to the countless ages that had shaped these subterranean realms. Stalactites hung like frozen tears from the ceilings, while stalagmites reached upwards like fingers seeking the light, creating a surreal landscape of natural sculptures that bore witness to the passage of millennia.

As Tiriaq and the Shadow Lion ventured deeper into the labyrinthine passages, they felt the weight of time pressing down upon them, a tangible reminder of the earth's enduring legacy and their fleeting presence within it. In the heart of these ancient caverns, they were but transient visitors, humbled by the vastness of the world and the mysteries it held.

Their journey through the ancient caverns led to Naji's village. As they ventured deeper into the labyrinthine passages, Tiriaq and the Shadow Lion navigated the twists and turns of the underground maze, guided by the faint echoes of Naji's voice and the distant flicker of torchlight.

The caverns presented a formidable challenge, with treacherous passages that seemed to shift and change with each step. Yet, fueled by their determination to find Naji and uncover the truth behind the Shadow Lion's cryptic messages, they pressed on, their resolve unshakable even in the face of uncertainty.

Chapter 12: Abyssal Altercations

Tiriaq and the Shadow Lion stumbled upon a scene of the cosmic conflict unfolding before them in the dimly lit depths of the caverns, where the air seemed to pulse with ancient energy. Beings adorned in armor that shimmered with the brilliance of starlight clashed amidst the cavernous expanse, their eyes gleaming with the intensity of their fervor for conquest. Each movement they made resonated with the echoes of ages past as they sought to harness the primordial energies of the underground realm for their nefarious ambitions.

These celestial beings, their forms contorted by the insatiable hunger for power, emerged as a dire threat not only to Tiriaq and the Shadow Lion but also to the delicate balance that governed the natural world. Their presence warped the very fabric of reality, casting a shadow of uncertainty over the once tranquil caverns. As they clashed in a symphony of cosmic chaos, the cavern walls trembled with the force of their conflict, threatening to collapse under the weight of their celestial fury.

For Tiriaq and the Shadow Lion, the sight was awe-inspiring and chilling as they realized the magnitude of the forces at play. With each clash of celestial steel, they felt the tremors reverberate through their very beings, a stark reminder of the perilous nature of their journey. Yet, amidst the chaos, they knew that they could not stand idly by while the delicate balance of the underground realm hung in the balance. With determination etched upon their faces, they braced themselves to confront the celestial adversaries before them, ready to defend the natural order at any cost.

With each step forward, the air crackled with tension, charged by the clash of opposing forces. The adversaries, their movements as swift as lightning, wielded the raw power of the caverns' ancient energies with a terrifying proficiency. Their luminous blades, forged from celestial essence, clashed against the shadows that enveloped Tiriaq and the Shadow Lion, casting flickering reflections against the rugged walls of the cavern.

As the battle raged on, the cavern echoed with the thunderous sound of metal meeting metal, reverberating through the subterranean expanse. The adversaries moved with an otherworldly grace, their forms illuminated by the ethereal glow of their weapons. Sparks danced in the darkness with each strike, painting a mesmerizing tableau of light and shadow upon the cavern floor.

Tiriaq and the Shadow Lion fought side by side; their movements synchronized perfectly. Together, they countered the onslaught of their celestial foes with a blend of skill and determination, their resolve unwavering in the face of overwhelming odds. Though the adversaries wielded the power of the ancient energies with formidable prowess, Tiriaq, and the Shadow Lion refused to yield, their spirits burning bright amidst the encroaching darkness.

Despite the overwhelming odds, Tiriaq and the Shadow Lion stood resolute, their spirits undaunted by the daunting challenge. With every strike and parry, they drew upon the strength of their bond and the knowledge they had acquired on their journey, determined to thwart the forces of light that sought to subjugate the underground realm.

Tiriaq wielded his old dagger with a newfound sense of purpose, its familiar weight a comforting reminder of his journey thus far. With each precise movement, he danced through the chaos of battle, his strikes guided by instinct and honed skill. Meanwhile, the Shadow Lion unleashed its formidable physicality, its lithe form weaving through the fray with a grace that belied its immense power.

Amidst the chaos of combat, Tiriaq was suddenly enveloped in a vision, the image of the Golden Lion shimmering before his eyes. In this moment of clarity, he glimpsed a path to victory, a revelation born from his connection to the ancient guardian. With renewed determination, Tiriaq channeled the essence of the Golden Lion, his movements infused with a divine energy that blazed like a beacon in the darkness.

As Tiriaq and the Shadow Lion fought side by side, their movements were a dance of synchronized grace amidst the chaotic clash. The cavern echoed with the clang of swords and the crackle of arcane energy as they battled against adversaries whose celestial forms shimmered with radiant power. Each strike and parry was met with a counter of equal force, the Shadow Lion's physical prowess complementing Tiriaq's agility and skill with his old dagger.

Amidst the tumult of combat, Tiriaq's mind raced with the intensity of the fight, yet amid the chaos, a subtle realization dawned upon him. The Shadow Lion's presence, unwavering support, and uncanny coordination in battle seemed to echo the essence of the legendary Golden Lion. It was as if the very spirit of the Golden Lion guided them, concealed within the shadowy form of Tiriaq's steadfast companion.

Despite the odds stacked against them, Tiriaq and the Shadow Lion pressed forward with unwavering determination. With each clash, they drew upon their shared strength, fueled by a bond forged through adversity and tempered in the fires of battle. Together, they pushed back against the celestial forces, inching closer to victory with every passing moment.

As the skirmish reached its climax, Tiriaq's vision blurred for a fleeting moment, and in that instant, he caught a glimpse of the elusive Golden Lion. Its radiant form shimmered amidst the chaos, a beacon of hope amidst the darkness, before fading into the shadows. With newfound resolve, Tiriaq and the Shadow Lion redoubled their efforts, driving back their adversaries with renewed vigor and determination.

With their adversaries vanquished and a moment of respite earned, Tiriaq and the Shadow Lion briefly paused to catch their breath. Each heaving breath seemed to reverberate through the cavern, a testament to the intensity of the battle they had just endured. As they gathered themselves, Tiriaq felt a surge of adrenaline coursing through his veins; his senses heightened, and his resolve was unwavering.

With determination etched upon their faces, Tiriaq and the Shadow Lion pressed onward, their footsteps echoing against the rugged walls of the cavern. Every twist and turn of the winding passages brought them closer to their destination, the torchlight flickering in the distance like a beacon guiding them through the darkness.

As they emerged into the vast chamber bathed in the soft glow of torchlight, Tiriaq's heart swelled with relief and anticipation. Ahead, nestled amidst the rocky alcoves, lay Naji's village, its humble structures offering a welcome respite from the harsh realities of the underground world. With its warm light and promise of companionship, the sight of the village filled Tiriaq with a sense of hope for the journey ahead.

Part 2: The Surface and the Secret

Chapter 13: An Evening of Tales and Bonds

As Tiriaq and the Shadow Lion stepped into the vast chamber, the soft glow of torchlight illuminated a scene that surpassed their expectations. Before them lay Naji's village, nestled among the rocky alcoves, its architecture seamlessly blending with the natural contours of the cavern. The village appeared like a hidden gem, a testament to human adaptability and resilience in the heart of the earth.

Naji's village nestled snugly within the rugged alcoves of the cavern, appearing almost as if it were a natural extension of the rocky landscape. The dwellings, constructed from a harmonious fusion of stone, wood, and woven vines, melded seamlessly with the cavern's natural contours. Some homes were built directly into the cavern walls, their facades adorned with intricate carvings depicting scenes from village life and ancient folklore.

The soft glow of torchlight cast gentle shadows across the village, illuminating the winding pathways that meandered between the clustered homes. Each path was lined with glowing lanterns crafted from delicate crystals, adding a touch of ethereal beauty to the village's rustic charm. Fragrant herbs and flowers spilled from wooden barrels and window boxes, infusing the air with their sweet scent and adding vibrant splashes of color to the earthy surroundings.

At the heart of the village, a central square opened up, serving as a communal gathering place for the villagers. A grand stone fountain stood here, its waters trickling down in a soothing melody that echoed through the cavern. Surrounding the fountain were sturdy wooden benches, where villagers would gather to socialize, share stories, and bask in the warmth of the community.

Despite being nestled deep within the earth, Naji's village exuded a sense of warmth and hospitality that was palpable to any visitor. It was a sanctuary amidst the darkness, a beacon of light and life in the depths of the cavernous expanse.

The villagers, accustomed to the quiet rhythm of their secluded life deep within the cavern, were caught off guard by the unexpected arrival of Tiriaq and the Shadow Lion. With hurried whispers and curious glances exchanged among them, they quickly gathered around, forming a semi-circle around the newcomers. Their faces reflected a mix of astonishment and reverence, their eyes wide with wonder at the sight before them.

With its luminous presence and regal demeanor, the Shadow Lion commanded the attention of all who beheld it. Its umbral fur seemed to shimmer in the torchlight, casting a mesmerizing aura that enveloped Tiriaq like a protective cloak. The villagers had heard tales of mythical creatures that roamed the lands above, but never in their wildest dreams did they imagine encountering one in their village.

Yet, despite their surprise, the villagers' demeanors reflected a sense of respect and admiration as they gazed upon Tiriaq and the Shadow Lion. They recognized the significance of this unexpected visit, sensing that it heralded something momentous. Some even felt a faint inkling of recognition stir within their hearts as if the arrival of these travelers held a more profound significance than they could comprehend.

For the villagers, who lived a life steeped in tradition and folklore, encountering Tiriaq and the Shadow Lion was like stepping into the pages of a long-forgotten legend. It was a rare and wondrous occasion that would be spoken of for generations to come. As they stood in silent awe, they eagerly awaited to hear the tale that had brought these extraordinary visitors to their humble village.

News of Tiriaq and the Shadow Lion's arrival spread like wildfire throughout the village, carrying on excited villagers' whispers as they hurriedly made their way to the square. Despite Naji's absence, the villagers were determined to welcome their unexpected guests warmly. With admirable efficiency, they set about preparing for a special evening in honor of Tiriaq and the Shadow Lion.

The village's central square was a hive of activity, bustling with villagers who had come together to celebrate the special evening. People of all ages mingled, their faces illuminated by the warm, flickering light of torches that lined the perimeter of the square. The aroma of roasted meats hung thick in the air, intermingling with the fragrance of freshly baked bread that wafted from nearby hearths.

In one corner of the square, a group of children chased each other around, their laughter echoing off the cavern walls. Nearby, elders sat in small clusters, engaged in animated conversations as they eagerly awaited the start of the storytelling event. The younger villagers helped to set up makeshift seating arrangements, arranging logs and stones around the central fire pit to create a cozy gathering space.

As the sun dipped below the horizon, casting its final rays across the cavern, the torches flickered to life, casting a soft, golden glow over the scene. The air was filled with anticipation as villagers settled into their seats, their faces aglow with excitement for the stories that were about to unfold.

In the center of the square, a makeshift stage was erected, its wooden platform bathed in the warm glow of torchlight. Here, under the watchful gaze of the cavern's ancient walls, the evening's festivities would unfold. As the villagers took their seats, their faces illuminated by the flickering flames, there was a palpable sense of excitement in the air. Tonight would be a night to remember, a testament to the bonds of friendship and the spirit of unity that bound them together.

Amidst the expectant crowd, an elder emerged, commanding attention as he stepped forward. His hair, as white as the moonlight that bathed the cavern, cascaded in wisps around his weathered face, and his eyes gleamed with a wisdom earned through a lifetime of experiences. With a dignified air, he raised his hand, signaling for silence as he prepared to address the gathered villagers.

In a voice that resonated with the depth of the earth itself, he began the evening of storytelling. "It began as thus," he intoned, his words carrying the weight of centuries-old wisdom. "In the time before time, when the world was young and the stars danced in the heavens, our ancestors roamed the vast expanse of the earth, seeking a place to call home. Guided by the whispers of the wind and the murmurs of the earth, they journeyed far and wide until they stumbled upon this sacred cavern, hidden away from the prying eyes of the world above."

"With hearts full of hope and hands hardened by toil, our ancestors set to work, carving out their new home from the very heart of the earth. They labored tirelessly, day and night, chiseling away at the rocky walls and shaping the cavern into a sanctuary fit for their descendants. With each swing of the pickaxe and each drop of sweat that fell to the ground, they infused the cavern with their love and dreams for the future."

"As the years passed and the village began to take shape, our ancestors faced many trials and tribulations. They battled against fierce storms threatening to flood their home and fierce beasts lurking in the darkness. Yet, through perseverance and determination, they overcame every obstacle that stood in their way, forging a bond with the land that would endure for generations to come."

"And so, in this very cavern, it was here that our village was born. It is a testament to the resilience of the human spirit and the enduring power of community. And though the world may change and time may march ever onward, the spirit of our ancestors, blessed by the whispers of the Goddess, lives on within every one of us, guiding us forward as we continue to write the story of our village's legacy."

As the elders recounted the tales of the village's history, Tiriaq listened intently, his eyes reflecting the flickering torchlight as he sat in silent rapture. The reverence with which the villagers spoke of The Goddess piqued his curiosity, yet he couldn't shake the feeling of unfamiliarity. They spoke of her as if she were a revered figure, guiding their ancestors through trials and tribulations, yet Tiriaq had never heard of her.

Despite his lack of knowledge about The Goddess, Tiriaq drew deeper into the stories, captivated by the vivid descriptions of her influence on the village's fate. Each word seemed to resonate with a truth that transcended his understanding, leaving him with a sense of wonder and reverence for the unseen forces that shaped the world around him.

Tiriaq recounted his journey to the attentive villagers with a humble yet determined voice. He described the chilling embrace of the frozen tundras, where the biting winds sculpted ice into ghostly forms, the lush valleys bursting with life, and rivers sang as they nurtured the land. He painted vivid pictures of ancient forests steeped in mystery, where the trees whispered secrets of ages past. With each word, he drew the villagers into his world, sharing the trials and triumphs of his odyssey.

As he spoke of the cosmic battle against seemingly celestial forces seeking to disrupt the world's balance, Tiriaq's voice resonated with conviction and courage. He spoke of the Shadow Lion, his steadfast companion in the face of adversity, and the unwavering bond that had guided them through their darkest hours. The villagers listened with rapt attention, hanging on every word as they marveled at the bravery and resilience of the young traveler and his mystical companion.

As Tiriaq delved into the tale of the Shadow Lion, a hush fell over the crowd, each villager leaning in eagerly. He spoke of the profound bond between himself and the enigmatic creature, a bond born in the crucible of adversity and tempered by mutual respect and affection. With earnest words, he described how they had faced insurmountable trials, drawing strength from each other and the fabric of the natural world.

As Tiriaq recounted the vision he had witnessed, a vision of the cosmic battle and the forces that threatened to disrupt the balance of the world, awe washed over the crowd. They listened in breathless silence, their hearts stirred by the young traveler's courage and the mystical revelations he shared. In that moment, Tiriaq's words transcended mere storytelling; they became a testament to the enduring power of resilience, friendship, and the unbreakable bond between humanity and nature.

As the evening of storytelling unfolded, it became more than just a series of tales; it transformed into a profound exchange of experiences and wisdom. Within the heart of the cavern, illuminated by the flickering torchlight, Tiriaq, and the villagers found common ground, bridging the gap between their worlds. Each story shared was a thread weaving together the fabric of their shared humanity, reminding them of the timeless power of storytelling to connect hearts and minds.

New bonds were forged under the earth's watchful gaze, surrounded by their ancestors' ancient echoes. These bonds were not superficial but rooted in mutual respect and the shared wonder of life's journey. In that sacred space, Tiriaq found himself welcomed into the embrace of a community that honored the wisdom of the past while embracing the promise of the future.

Chapter 14: On the Precipice

In the tranquil embrace of early morning, as the first tendrils of light crept across the sky, bathing the cavern's expansive walls in a soft palette of gold and amber, Tiriaq found himself meandering near the village's periphery. He was captivated by the unspoiled beauty that lay just beyond the settlement's bounds, where nature whispered secrets carried by the wind. He encountered a remarkable presence in this moment of quiet reflection amidst a symphony of birds heralding the dawn and the soothing susurrus of the breeze through the leaves.

A figure stepped forth from the concealment of the underbrush, moving with a confidence that seemed to command the very earth he walked upon. Yet, for all his assertive stride, there was a hint of weariness about him, as if he bore the weight of countless unseen burdens. The rising sun cast elongated shadows that trailed behind him, mirroring his steps in the early light. This man was of moderate stature, yet his bearing suggested a life shaped by relentless toil and perseverance. The strands of his hair, woven with streaks of gray, told tales not of advancing age but of experiences rich and varied. His skin, etched with lines and kissed by the sun, was a testament to years spent under open skies against the backdrop of stars.

However, what truly captivated Tiriaq, drawing him in with an almost magnetic pull, were the man's eyes. They were deep pools of insight and understanding, glowing with an intensity that seemed to pierce through to the very soul. Within their depths were stories of laughter and tears, triumphs and tribulations, swirled together, offering a glimpse into a life of profound depth and complexity. These were not the eyes of an ordinary man; they were windows to a spirit that had tasted the full spectrum of human emotion, bearing wisdom gleaned from a myriad of experiences.

As Tiriaq stood there, momentarily transfixed by the sight before him, he felt an inexplicable connection to this stranger. It was as though, in a few heartbeats, he had stumbled upon a living embodiment of the land itself—rugged, enduring, and immeasurably deep.

In the man's grasp, carefully cradled as if it were a treasure of immense value, was a basket skillfully crafted from the supple branches of the local flora. It was modest in size but held within it the essence of the forest itself. Over its top, a cloth was gently laid, concealing the bounty it contained. Despite this veil, the air around him was imbued with the vibrant aroma of freshly gathered herbs. These earthy and potent scents seemed to weave a narrative of their own—one of rejuvenation, of the meticulous care with which the earth tends to its inhabitants.

As he progressed with deliberate steps towards the village's pulsating heart, the soft rustling of leaves underfoot accompanied his journey. This commonplace yet infinitely comforting sound spoke of a day awakening to its full potential, of life persisting in its most sincere form. Yet, for all the noise he made, the man seemed unaware of Tiriaq's watchful eyes, his focus undivided as he neared his destination.

Driven by an insatiable curiosity and a desire to bridge the gap between them, Tiriaq made his decision. He stepped forward, emerging from the observer's role into that of an active participant in this early morning encounter. "Greetings," he ventured, his voice slicing through the serene silence that had blanketed their surroundings. It was a simple word, a universal token of peace, yet it carried the weight of his intentions.

At the sound of Tiriaq's voice, the man abruptly stopped. There was a palpable shift in his demeanor; the relaxed assurance that had characterized his movements gave way to a heightened alertness. He turned, his body adopting a stance that spoke of readiness, of a life conditioned to anticipate the unexpected. The warmth and open hospitality that had so defined Tiriaq's welcome by the village seemed, in that instant, to be worlds away. Instead, he was met with a look of measured caution, a scrutiny that seemed to probe the essence of his being.

This change, this sudden introduction of distance where there had been none, left Tiriaq momentarily adrift. The open faces and smiling welcomes that had greeted him upon his arrival had not prepared him for this. It was a reminder that trust was a commodity earned, not freely given and that the warmth of a community did not necessarily extend to every individual within it unconditionally.

"You're the traveler, then," Naji declared, his statement hanging between them like a carefully placed question, yet his tone left no room for doubt. It was not a query but a confirmation of what he already suspected. "The one who arrived with the Shadow Lion." His voice, though steady, carried an undercurrent of solemnity as if the very mention of the Shadow Lion added weight to his words.

For a moment, Tiriaq felt as though he had been placed under a microscope, his every intention and past action scrutinized through Naji's discerning gaze. "Yes, I am Tiriaq," he responded, striving to bridge the gap of uncertainty with a gesture of goodwill. He extended his hand, an offering of peace in a moment teetering on the brink of mistrust.

Naji's eyes lingered on Tiriaq's outstretched hand, a silent war of judgment and acceptance playing out in their depths before he finally decided to take it. The handshake was brief but revealing; Naji's grip was firm, and the texture of his palm was a testament to a life marked by resilience and labor. "I am Naji," he introduced himself, the title of 'village leader' carried with an air of humble authority rather than pride. "And these," he motioned towards the basket he carried, now a symbol of his dedication, "are healing herbs for one of our own who's fallen ill."

The mention of the ill villager momentarily shifted the conversation's focus, allowing Tiriaq to glimpse the fabric of the community and its interwoven sense of responsibility and care. However, his admission quickly realigned his thoughts. "I didn't expect such a cautious reception," Tiriaq confessed, his eyes momentarily drifting towards the village, a beacon of warmth and acceptance that now felt miles away.

Naji's gaze followed Tiriaq's, then returned to the Shadow Lion, acknowledging the creature with a nod that seemed to carry centuries of wisdom. "How else can I be, for the bearer of An End or A Beginning?" His words, cryptic and loaded with unspoken knowledge, hung in the air like a challenge or an invitation to uncover more profound truths.

Tiriaq was momentarily speechless, the gravity of Naji's statement anchoring him to the spot. An End or A Beginning—phrases that hinted at prophecies untold and fates intertwined. What knowledge did Naji possess that led him to view their arrival with such a dual perspective? Was he aware of the island's prophecy, or did his insight plunge deeper into a well of secrets Tiriaq had yet to comprehend?

The realization that his journey was entangled with mysteries far more significant than he had anticipated washed over Tiriaq. It was a moment of reckoning, a silent acknowledgment that the path he walked was mapped with signs and omens understood by few. With his guarded welcome and veiled references, Naji had just expanded the horizon of Tiriaq's quest, hinting at a narrative far broader and more intricate than a mere traveler and his mystical companion could have imagined.

In that moment of revelation, the world around Tiriaq seemed to pause, the early morning's gentle breeze and the distant calls of the waking birds fading into a hushed silence. Naji's words, "An End or A Beginning," echoed in the chambers of Tiriaq's mind, each syllable heavy with the promise of destinies yet to unfold. These were not merely words; they were keys to understanding the intricate tapestry of the world's unseen forces, spoken by someone who had glimpsed its frayed edges and hidden patterns.

Tiriaq's heart raced as he contemplated the depths of Naji's knowledge. How had this village leader, a guardian of a seemingly secluded community, come to possess insights that felt as ancient as the earth itself? In his years of stewardship, could Naji have encountered signs, omens, or artifacts that spoke of the larger forces at play in the world—forces that Tiriaq and the Shadow Lion were now unwittingly a part of?

The duality of Naji's statement—An End or A Beginning—suggested a pivotal role that Tiriaq and his companion might play in the unfolding events. It hinted at a crossroads in the cosmic balance, where their actions could tip the scales towards renewal or ruin. This realization was both exhilarating and daunting. Tiriaq wondered if the island's prophecy, whispered in the winds and sung by the seas, was but a single thread in a grander weave of destinies intertwined. Did Naji see the harbingers of change in them, or did he perceive a deeper, more personal connection to the prophecy that Tiriaq himself was yet to uncover?

With a mind swirling with questions and a heart heavy with newfound responsibility, Tiriaq looked into Naji's eyes, seeking answers or perhaps guidance. There was an unspoken understanding between them, recognizing the journey's weight and the choices ahead. Tiriaq realized that their meeting was not by chance but a confluence of paths meant to cross at this critical juncture. The wisdom that Naji held, veiled in his guarded words and cautious welcome, was a beacon for Tiriaq, illuminating the first steps towards unraveling the mysteries that lay woven into his destiny.

Naji's gaze held Tiriaq's, unflinching, as the silence stretched between them, thick with unvoiced secrets and the weight of histories yet to be written. Finally, the village leader spoke, his voice softer now yet imbued with an earnest gravity that commanded attention. "Amaruq's son," he murmured, a hint of respect threading through his words. "Then, you carry not only the legacy of your father but perhaps the fate of us all upon your shoulders."

He paused as if weighing the wisdom of his following words before continuing. "The prophecy, spoken of in hushed tones since the time of my ancestors, tells of journeyers allied with the embodiment of primal spirits. It is said this alliance will stand at the crossroads of our world's destiny, wielding the power to usher in an era of unprecedented peace or cast us down into unending turmoil."

Naji's eyes searched Tiriaq's, seeking signs of understanding, of acceptance. "Your arrival with the

Shadow Lion has stirred the hearts of our people and ignited hope amid our quiet lives. But hope is a double-edged sword, Tiriaq. It can lead us to salvation or into the depths of despair."

Tiriaq felt the weight of Naji's words settle upon him like a mantle. Once a distant legend, the prophecy felt intimately connected to his path. The choices he would make and the challenges he would face all seemed to converge toward a destiny he was only beginning to understand.

"Please, tell me," Tiriaq implored, his voice a whisper against the dawn's light. "How can I ensure that my journey, our journey, leads to peace? How can I carry this responsibility and not falter?"

Naji looked at Tiriaq, a measure of reassurance entering his gaze. "The path is not for me to dictate, nor the outcome for me to foresee. Your heart will be your compass, guided by the wisdom of those who walk beside you and the lessons of those who walked before. The balance you seek, the choice between an end and a beginning, lies within the courage to face the unknown, to embrace the lessons of the past while forging a new path forward."

As their profound exchange dwindled to a thoughtful silence, Naji shifted, breaking the moment's intensity with a simple yet meaningful gesture. He lifted the basket of herbs slightly as if weighing its significance, then extended an invitation with a nod toward the path that led deeper into the village. "Come," he said, his voice now imbued with a warmth that seemed to bridge the gap their previous conversation had created. "Walk with me. These herbs won't deliver themselves, and I believe our talk is far from over." His eyes twinkled with an unspoken promise of continued guidance and shared purpose. Tiriaq, feeling a renewed sense of camaraderie and curiosity, nodded in agreement.

Chapter 15: The Legacy of Light and Shadow

"It began as thus," Naji's voice carried a reverence that immediately enveloped them in a shroud of anticipation and respect. "Our world, as vast and as beautiful as it is now, was not the first iteration of creation. The annals of our history, preserved through oral tradition, speak of a time before, a world that existed in a form unrecognizable to us now."

Naji's words hung in the air like a sacred incantation, drawing Tiriaq deeper into the narrative unfolding before him. With each syllable, the weight of ages past seemed to settle upon them, infusing the cavern's atmosphere with an aura of ancient wisdom. Tiriaq felt a stirring in his soul, a primal connection to the stories of his ancestors and the mysteries that lay veiled within the fabric of time itself.

He paused, allowing the weight of his words to sink in, then continued, "Into this primeval chaos, The Goddess emerged. She was a beacon of hope for those who sought refuge from the unforgiving surface. With her, a magnificent creature of Light and Shadow, embodying the balance of all existence."

Naji's voice carried a profound reverence as he spoke of The Goddess, each syllable resonating with the ancient wisdom passed down through generations. Tiriaq listened intently, his imagination painting vivid pictures of this divine figure and her enigmatic companion. In his mind's eye, he could almost see The Goddess, her form radiant with ethereal light, standing alongside the creature that embodied the delicate dance between light and shadow. The image filled him with awe and wonder, a testament to the enduring power of myth and legend in shaping the collective consciousness of a people.

Tiriaq's mind raced, images of the Shadow Lion flashing before his eyes, a creature that seemed to walk the line between legend and reality. As Naji spoke of The Goddess and her mystical companion, Tiriaq couldn't shake the uncanny resemblance between the Shadow Lion and the creature described in the ancient tale. Was it mere coincidence, or was there a deeper connection between his enigmatic companion and the legendary figure of The Goddess? The thought shivered down Tiriaq's spine, stirring excitement and apprehension.

Naji went on, "Together, they guided our ancestors to these caverns, revealing the secrets of living beneath the earth, in harmony with its heartbeat. The Goddess showed them how to draw water from the stone, cultivate food without the sun's direct kiss, and harness the earth's energy for warmth and light. It was a time of great transformation, as our people learned to coexist with the natural rhythms of the underground world, forging a bond with the land that would endure for generations to come."

"The Goddess's teachings were not just of survival, but of thriving in balance with the unseen forces that weave the tapestry of life. But," Naji's tone shifted, a shadow crossing his features, "she left us with a prophecy—a warning. Harbingers would come, she said, bearers of change. These harbingers would herald a new age, an era of unparalleled prosperity or destruction. The Beginning of a New World, or the End of all we know. And so, our ancestors passed down this knowledge through the generations, a reminder of the delicate balance we must maintain and the vigilance required to safeguard our way of life."

Tiriaq felt a shiver run down his spine as he absorbed Naji's words. The prophecy seemed to echo his journey, the mysterious connection with the Shadow Lion, and the unforeseen path before them. It was as though the threads of fate were weaving around him, pulling him deeper into a story that transcended his understanding. The weight of responsibility settled upon his shoulders, mingling with a sense of awe and trepidation at the magnitude of the task ahead.

"Your arrival, with a creature of Shadow by your side, has stirred the hearts of many in our village," Naji confessed, his gaze fixed on Tiriaq with an intensity that seemed to peer into his soul. "Some see it as a sign of hope, the dawn of a new era. Others fear it may signal the end of our days. There are whispers among the elders; tales passed down through generations, that speak of such times when the balance of the world teeters on the edge of a knife. Your presence here, Tiriaq, may hold the key to unlocking the mysteries of our past and shaping the destiny of our future."

Chapter 16: A Retrospective

As they arrived at the villager's dwelling, a sense of quiet urgency hung in the air, contrasting with the serene beauty of the cavernous surroundings. The humble abode, crafted from stone and earth, seemed to blend seamlessly with the natural contours of the cavern walls, a testament to the villagers' harmonious existence with their environment. Naji's ordinarily calm demeanor was now marked by a palpable determination, evident in his jaw set and the focused intensity of his gaze. With a silent nod of assurance to Tiriaq, he motioned for the traveler to wait outside, a quiet acknowledgment of the sanctity of the healing process about to unfold within the dwelling.

As Naji disappeared into the dim interior of the dwelling, Tiriaq found himself momentarily alone amidst the tranquil stillness of the village outskirts. The morning sunlight filtered through the canopy of rocky overhangs, casting dappled patterns of light and shadow on the rugged terrain below. The soft rustle of leaves and the distant hum of village life provided a soothing backdrop to the scene, offering a moment of respite amidst the weighty contemplations swirling in Tiriaq's mind.

Outside the dwelling, Tiriaq stood in silent vigil, his senses keenly attuned to the subtle rhythms of the surrounding environment. The cool touch of the cavern walls against his skin reminded him of the ancient wisdom permeating this subterranean world's fabric. With each passing moment, anticipation mounted, mingling with reverence for the healing rituals unfolding within the confines of the humble abode.

Minutes stretched into hours as Tiriaq waited patiently, the passage of time marked by the shifting play of light and shadow across the rocky landscape. The steady rhythm of his breaths mirrored the ebb and flow of life itself, a quiet reminder of the interconnectedness of all beings and the delicate balance that sustained their existence. Amidst the tranquility of the village outskirts, Tiriaq found himself drawn into a state of introspection, contemplating the mysteries of the universe and his place within it.

Left to his own devices, Tiriaq stood amidst the tranquil outskirts of the village, where the earth seemed to breathe in harmony with the rhythms of life. The morning sun, a radiant orb of golden light, painted the rugged terrain with hues of amber and ochre, casting long, stretching shadows that danced across the rocky landscape. Each contour and crevice of the cavern walls was illuminated with a soft, ethereal glow, lending an air of mystique to the surroundings.

As Tiriaq surveyed the tranquil scene, he couldn't help but be captivated by the interplay of light and shadow, a timeless dance that mirrored the complexities of his thoughts. The gentle rustle of leaves, stirred by a subtle breeze, added a melodic cadence to the stillness, punctuating the silence with nature's gentle whispers. In the distance, the muted sounds of village life echoed faintly, a reminder of the bustling activity just beyond the village outskirts.

In the embrace of the morning's serenity, Tiriaq immersed himself in a profound sense of introspection, his thoughts drifting like wisps of smoke on the gentle currents of the breeze. With each breath, he felt a deep connection to the ancient wisdom that permeated the very fabric of the earth, a reminder of the interconnectedness of all living beings and the timeless rhythms of the natural world. Amidst the tranquility of the village outskirts, Tiriaq found solace in the quiet solitude, a moment of respite amidst the tumultuous journey ahead.

Alone with his thoughts, Tiriaq was ensconced in a cocoon of introspection, the weight of Naji's words pressing upon him like a heavy cloak. The gravity of the village's ancient prophecy hung heavy in the air, its implications weaving a tangled web of uncertainty and foreboding in Tiriaq's mind.

Lost amidst the labyrinth of his thoughts, Tiriaq paced with measured steps, his footfalls echoing softly against the cavern walls. Each stride seemed to carry him deeper into the recesses of his consciousness, where the boundaries between reality and legend blurred into obscurity.

As he wrestled with the enigma of his existence, Tiriaq's mind became a tempest of conflicting emotions and unanswered questions. What role did he genuinely play in the grand tapestry of fate? Was he but a mere pawn in a cosmic game of destiny, or did he possess the agency to carve his path amidst the tumult of unfolding events?

With furrowed brow and furled lips, Tiriaq grappled with the weight of responsibility that now lay upon his shoulders. The specter of uncertainty loomed large in his mind, casting doubt over his every thought and action. Yet, amidst the swirling maelstrom of his misgivings, a flicker of determination burned bright within him, a steadfast resolve to confront whatever trials lay ahead and emerge victorious against all odds.

As the hours trickled by, the sun ascended its celestial arc, painting the village in hues of golden radiance and banishing the lingering specters of doubt that had clouded Tiriaq's mind. Lost in the labyrinth of his ruminations, Tiriaq stood like a solitary sentinel, his gaze fixed upon the horizon as he awaited Naji's imminent return.

With each passing moment, the village seemed to awaken from its slumber, the gentle hum of activity gradually crescendoing into a symphony of bustling life. From the nearby hearths, the tantalizing aroma of hearty prepared meals wafted into the air, mingling with the fragrant scents of wildflowers.

Lost in the ebb and flow of the village's daily rhythms, Tiriaq remained entrenched in his reverie, the weight of impending destiny bearing upon his shoulders like an unyielding burden. Yet, despite the tumult of emotions that churned within him, there lingered a quiet sense of anticipation, a silent acknowledgment of the mysteries that awaited him beyond the threshold of the present moment.

Suddenly, the unmistakable sounds of jubilation emanating from the village's entrance shattered the morning's tranquility. Tiriaq's curiosity piqued, he turned his gaze towards the source of the commotion, wondering who could have arrived now to elicit such a warm welcome from the villagers.

Chapter 17: The Path to Understanding

As Ayuka and the Golden Lion stumbled upon a caravan of traders, their hearts swelled with excitement and curiosity. The ragtag assembly of the trading expedition was a sight to behold—a vibrant tapestry of seasoned merchants with stories etched into their faces and curious adventurers whose eyes sparkled with the thrill of the unknown. They greeted Ayuka and her majestic companion with a warmth that felt like a balm to their travel-weary souls, their fascination with the Golden Lion palpable in their eager, welcoming gestures.

The journey with the caravan unfurled like a vivid dream, taking Ayuka and the Golden Lion through landscapes so mesmerizing that they seemed to leap straight out of the ancient tales Ayuka had grown up listening to. Each twist and turn of their path unveiled natural wonders that filled her with delight and surprise. They traversed dense, whispering forests where the air was thick with mystery, crossed babbling streams that sparkled under the sun's caress, and navigated rolling meadows dotted with wildflowers whose colors painted the horizon in hues of endless possibilities.

For Ayuka, every landscape was a chapter of discovery, a series of lessons in the beauty and diversity of the world beyond her wildest imagination. She watched in awe as the caravan maneuvered through these varied terrains, adapting to each new challenge with a resilience that inspired her. The camaraderie among the traders, their shared laughter, and stories around the campfire at night added layers of richness to the journey that Ayuka hadn't anticipated. It was a mosaic of human spirit and adventure, of bonds formed in the crucible of shared experiences.

The golden lion, too, seemed to thrive in this ever-changing environment, bringing a sense of majesty and wonder to the caravan. Its golden mane glinted in the sunlight as it walked beside Ayuka, a silent guardian whose aura whispered ancient magic and untold stories. To the traders and adventurers, the golden lion was a symbol of the extraordinary, a living legend that walked among them, adding an element of awe to their everyday realities.

As the caravan meandered through the diverse tapestry of landscapes, the traders, seasoned by countless journeys and rich in the lore of the lands they traversed, began to weave tales that captured Ayuka's imagination. Their stories, with the reverence of those who have witnessed the world's wonders, painted vivid pictures of Naji's village—a place where the veil between the mundane and the magical seemed almost nonexistent. They described a community deeply rooted in tradition, where magic wasn't just a part of everyday life but intertwined with the very fabric of their existence.

Naji emerged in their tales as a figure of near-mythical stature, a guardian of ancient knowledge, and a benevolent force for good. His wisdom was said to be vast, encompassing the lore of the land, the language of the elements, and the secrets of the stars. The traders recounted stories of his kindness, how he welcomed all who sought his guidance, offering shelter and wisdom to those who approached him with respect and an open heart. His reputation painted him not just as a leader but as a bridge between the old ways and the ever-unfolding journey of life, making him a beacon for seekers of truth and knowledge.

As described by the traders, the village itself held a unique position in the world. It was a sanctuary for the mystic arts, a haven where the earth's ancient energies were acknowledged and celebrated. They spoke of ceremonies that called upon the forces of nature, rituals that honored the moon's cycles, and a deep, harmonious relationship with the natural world that seemed almost forgotten in other parts of the world. This place, where tradition and magic danced in unbroken unity, promised answers to the questions that burned in Ayuka's heart.

These stories ignited a flame of longing within Ayuka, a desire to delve deeper into the mysteries of her bond with the Golden Lion and to understand the ancient energies that whispered to her soul. The traders' tales suggested that the answers she sought might be found in Naji's village, in the teachings of Naji himself, or perhaps in the very air and soil of that enchanted place. The prospect of uncovering the connections between her destiny, the Golden Lion's legacy, and the mystical traditions of Naji's village filled her with a sense of purpose and a deep yearning to bridge the gap between her nascent abilities and the land's ancient wisdom.

Throughout the journey, Ayuka became an avid student of the traders' craft, seizing every moment as an opportunity to expand her knowledge and understanding of the world around her. The caravan, a microcosm of society with its intricate web of relationships, offered her a unique vantage point from which to observe the subtleties of human interaction and the complexities of commerce that bound these diverse communities together.

She watched closely as the traders engaged in negotiations, noting the careful choice of words, the strategic pauses, and the respectful nods punctuating their conversations. Ayuka marveled at their skill in striking a delicate balance between firmness and flexibility, asserting their needs while accommodating those of their counterparts. This dance of diplomacy, as nuanced and varied as the lands they traversed, revealed the depth of understanding and mutual respect required to forge lasting alliances.

As the caravan wound through bustling marketplaces and quiet villages, Ayuka observed the traders' interactions with the locals. She was fascinated by how they adapted their approach to suit each community, employing humor and humility in one place and reverence and formality in another. This adaptability, Ayuka realized, was born of a deep respect for the cultures and traditions they encountered, a cornerstone of successful trade and peaceful coexistence.

As the caravan journeyed towards Naji's village, Ayuka marveled at the traders' unwavering determination in adversity. Not only did they confront the harsh elements of nature, but they also grappled with supernatural forces that sought to hinder their progress. Dark shadows loomed ominously at the forest's edge, their malevolent whispers chilling Ayuka to the bone. It seemed as though these shadows were agents of the Shadows themselves, weaving spells of darkness to impede the caravan's advance.

However, amidst the darkness and uncertainty, Ayuka couldn't help but notice the remarkable resilience of the traders. Despite the looming threat, they pressed on with unwavering resolve, their spirits undaunted by the shadows surrounding them. What struck Ayuka even more was how the Golden Lion seemed to guide them through the darkness, its shadowy presence hinting at hidden depths of power and knowledge. It was as though the lion's presence imbued the caravan with an otherworldly strength, leading them through the shadowy labyrinth with an almost supernatural grace.

Inspired by the traders' steadfastness and the Golden Lion's mysterious guidance, Ayuka felt her resolve growing with each step they took. She realized that in the face of adversity, true strength lay not in the absence of fear but in the courage to confront it head-on. Through their shared struggles, Ayuka discovered a newfound sense of purpose and determination, drawing strength from the bond she shared with the Golden Lion and the camaraderie of her fellow travelers.

From the traders, Ayuka gleaned invaluable insights into the art of diplomacy and the intricacies of trade. She understood that these skills were not merely about negotiation and commerce but were fundamental to building relationships, resolving conflicts, and fostering a sense of community among disparate peoples. This knowledge, Ayuka sensed, would be crucial in the times ahead as she sought to navigate the challenges of her journey and fulfill her destiny.

This immersive education in the ways of the world, coupled with the deepening connection to the Golden Lion, enriched Ayuka's perspective, equipping her with the tools she would need to face the future. The lessons learned on the road with the traders became a foundational part of her growth, preparing her for the complex tapestry of interactions and decisions ahead in her quest to understand the mysteries of her bond and the ancient energies that flowed through the land.

With each day that passed on their journey toward Naji's village, Ayuka and the Golden Lion witnessed a transformation in the world around them. The endless expanse of arid desert gradually receded, replaced by a vibrant tapestry of life and color. Rolling hills unfurled beneath the azure sky, dotted with wildflowers that danced in the gentle breeze. Verdant valleys cradled streams of water so clearly, that they seemed more like streams of light, meandering through forests lush with the promise of endless mysteries. The air, once heavy with the heat of the desert, now carried the sweet fragrance of flowering plants, mingling with the melodious symphony of birdsong. This harmonious blend of sights, sounds, and scents was more than just a change in scenery; it was a testament to life's resilience and the natural world's boundless beauty.

As they ventured deeper into this newfound paradise, the transformation of the landscape became a mirror of the change within Ayuka herself. The harshness of the desert had tested them and tempered their spirits, but here, amidst the abundance of life, Ayuka found a profound sense of peace. The beauty of the land soothed her soul, reminding her why their journey mattered. It was a stark contrast to the desolation they had left behind, highlighting the importance of their mission—to preserve the delicate balance that allowed such beauty to flourish.

The traders' tales vividly depicted Naji's village, portraying it as a beacon of mystic arts and reverence for the natural world. It stood apart from other settlements as a community and a living testament to the profound connection between humanity and the earth. They spoke of ancient ceremonies that invoked the elemental forces, where the very earth seemed to pulse with life in response to the villagers' chants and offerings. These rituals were not mere superstitions but deeply ingrained traditions that honored the rhythms of nature, from the waxing and waning of the moon to the changing of the seasons.

In Naji's village, the villagers lived in harmony with the land, their lives intertwined with the ebb and flow of the natural world. They cultivated a deep respect for the earth and all its inhabitants, viewing themselves not as masters of the land but as its custodians. This reverence extended beyond mere words or rituals; it was ingrained in daily life, from how they tended their crops to the songs they sang under the starlit sky.

As Ayuka listened to these tales, a sense of wonder and longing stirred within her. She had always felt a deep connection to the natural world, a calling that whispered to her soul with every rustle of the leaves and every ripple on the water. In Naji's village, she sensed a kindred spirit where her affinity for nature would be accepted and embraced.

The traders' descriptions painted a vibrant tapestry of life in Naji's village, where every stone, every tree, and every creature held a story waiting to be told. It was a place of ancient wisdom and timeless beauty, a sanctuary where the mysteries of the earth were revered and celebrated. For Ayuka, it was more than just a destination; it was a journey of self-discovery, a quest to unlock the secrets of her connection to the natural world.

The tales spun by the traders ignited a fervent longing within Ayuka, a yearning that resonated deep within her being. It was a yearning for knowledge and understanding, a thirst to unravel the threads of destiny that bound her to the Golden Lion and the ancient energies that coursed through her veins. As the caravan pressed onward toward Naji's village, Ayuka was consumed by the tantalizing prospect of uncovering the hidden secrets within its hallowed halls. She imagined herself standing before Naji, the venerable sage whose wisdom was said to rival that of the earth itself, eager to absorb every word, every gesture, every nuance of his teachings.

With each step closer to their destination, Ayuka's anticipation grew, her mind buzzing with questions and possibilities. What truths awaited her in the depths of Naji's village? What mysteries lay concealed within its labyrinthine tunnels and sacred groves? The traders' tales had hinted at a legacy as old as time itself, a legacy that spoke to the very heart of Ayuka's existence. She longed to unlock the secrets of her bond with the Golden Lion, to delve into the depths of her soul and emerge, reborn and enlightened, into a world where the boundaries between the mundane and the magical blurred and faded away.

In the quiet moments of the journey, as the caravan wound through sun-dappled forests and rugged mountain passes, Ayuka was lost in contemplation. She traced the contours of the Golden Lion's fur with gentle fingers, feeling the steady thrum of its presence beside her. Together, they embarked on a quest to test their courage, resilience, and unwavering bond. But Ayuka knew, deep down in her heart, that it was a quest worth undertaking, for it held the promise of discovery, enlightenment, and a destiny writ large upon the tapestry of the cosmos. The tales spun by the traders ignited a fervent longing within Ayuka, a yearning that resonated deep within her being. It was a yearning for knowledge and understanding, a thirst to unravel the threads of destiny that bound her to the Golden Lion and the ancient energies that coursed through her veins. As the caravan pressed onward toward Naji's village, Ayuka was consumed by the tantalizing prospect of uncovering the hidden secrets within its hallowed halls. She imagined herself standing before Naji, the venerable sage whose wisdom was said to rival that of the earth itself, eager to absorb every word, every gesture, every nuance of his teachings.

With each step closer to their destination, Ayuka's anticipation grew, her mind buzzing with questions and possibilities. What truths awaited her in the depths of Naji's village? What mysteries lay concealed within its labyrinthine tunnels and sacred groves? The traders' tales had hinted at a legacy as old as time itself, a legacy that spoke to the very heart of Ayuka's existence. She longed to unlock the secrets of her bond with the Golden Lion, to delve into the depths of her soul and emerge, reborn and enlightened, into a world where the boundaries between the mundane and the magical blurred and faded away.

In the quiet moments of the journey, as the caravan wound through sun-dappled forests and rugged mountain passes, Ayuka was lost in contemplation. She traced the contours of the Golden Lion's fur with gentle fingers, feeling the steady thrum of its presence beside her. Together, they embarked on a quest to test their courage, resilience, and unwavering bond. But Ayuka knew, deep down in her heart, that it was a quest worth undertaking, for it held the promise of discovery, enlightenment, and a destiny writ large upon the tapestry of the cosmos.

Approaching the location of Naji's village, their path took an unexpected turn. The earth opened before them, revealing a vast cavern that beckoned them into its depths. As they descended, the daylight faded, giving way to a serene twilight that enveloped the cavern. Here, the air was cool and filled with the subtle music of dripping water, the sound echoing softly off the stone walls. Bioluminescent fungi cast a gentle glow, painting the cavern in hues of blue and green, illuminating the way forward.

This underground world was a stark departure from the vibrant life above, yet it held its form of beauty. Stalactites and stalagmites jutted from the ground and ceiling, natural sculptures carved by time. Small pools of water reflected the ethereal light, creating the illusion of stars shining beneath their feet. The path, now a winding trail through the heart of the earth, led them directly toward the hidden village of Naji.

Entering the underground village was like stepping into another world. The cavern opened into a sprawling network of tunnels and chambers, each skillfully crafted to harmonize with the cave's natural architecture. The villagers had turned this subterranean expanse into a sanctuary, a testament to their respect for the land and ability to adapt to its challenges.

For Ayuka, the journey from the harsh desert, through the verdant valleys, and into the heart of the earth was a powerful reminder of the diversity and resilience of the natural world. It reinforced her commitment to her mission, solidifying her resolve to protect the balance of nature. She hoped to find wisdom, allies, and the strength to face the challenges ahead in this underground haven.

Chapter 18: An Unexpected Meeting

Ayuka's heart swelled with joy as the caravan finally arrived at Naji's village, nestled deep within the labyrinthine tunnels of the underground cavern. Despite the subterranean setting, the village radiated warmth and vibrancy, illuminated by glowing crystals embedded in the cavern walls that cast a soft, ethereal light over the festivities. As Ayuka stepped off the caravan, she was enveloped by the welcoming embrace of the villagers, their smiles as bright as the lanterns that lined the pathways. They greeted her with open arms, their voices a melodic chorus of welcome that echoed through the cavernous expanse. It was a celebration unlike any Ayuka had ever seen, a harmonious blend of tradition and modernity, where ancient customs were honored alongside innovative technologies born of necessity. In the midst of it all, Ayuka felt a sense of belonging that went beyond mere words, as if she had finally found a home amidst the hidden depths of the earth.

As she stepped off the caravan, Ayuka was met with cheers and applause from the villagers, their faces alight with excitement and curiosity. They marveled at the sight of the Golden Lion by her side, its majestic presence casting a radiant glow illuminating the village. Children darted around her, their laughter echoing off the cavern walls as they gazed in awe at the magnificent creature. Ayuka couldn't help but feel a sense of pride as she introduced herself to the villagers, her bond with the Golden Lion shining like a beacon of hope amidst the darkness. Elders approached her, their eyes filled with wisdom and reverence, as they whispered words of welcome and admiration for her remarkable connection to the Golden Lion. It was a moment of pure magic, a merging of ancient tradition and modern marvel, that left Ayuka feeling humbled and honored to be embraced by the community in such a profound way.

Throughout the day, Ayuka was showered with gifts and accolades and welcomed into the heart of the village with open arms. The villagers told her tales of their bonds with familiars, sharing stories of courage, loyalty, and sacrifice. Ayuka listened with rapt attention, eager to learn more about the rich tapestry of life in Naji's village and the ancient traditions that bound its people together. She sat among them, her eyes sparkling with curiosity as elders recounted legends of heroes and mythical creatures, each tale weaving a spell of wonder and enchantment around her. As the day unfolded, Ayuka was immersed in the vibrant tapestry of village life, from the bustling marketplace where merchants bartered for goods to the tranquil gardens where healers tended to the sick and weary. Everywhere she turned, she encountered kindness and generosity, a testament to the spirit of community that thrived within the village's underground sanctuary.

As the sun descended beyond the horizon, casting hues of orange and pink across the sky, the villagers gathered in the central square for a feast in Ayuka's honor. Tables adorned with colorful flowers and flickering candles stretched as far as the eye could see, groaning under the weight of delicious foods and exotic delicacies brought from far and wide. Musicians played lively tunes on traditional instruments, their melodies weaving through the air and beckoning villagers to dance and rejoice.

Ayuka was swept up in the festivities, her laughter mingling with the joyful sounds of the celebration. Villagers of all ages joined hands and danced in circles, their faces radiant with smiles as they moved to the rhythm of the music. Children chased each other through the crowd, their laughter echoing off the cavern walls, while elders shared tales of times long past, their voices filled with wisdom and nostalgia.

Throughout the evening, Ayuka was approached by villagers eager to welcome her into their community. They offered her blessings and well-wishes, expressing their gratitude for her presence and the light she brought with her. Some shared gifts of handmade crafts and intricate jewelry, tokens of their appreciation for her role in safeguarding the balance of the natural world.

The festivities reached a crescendo of joy and merriment as the night wore on and the stars twinkled overhead. Newfound friends surrounded Ayuka, their bonds forged in the warmth of shared laughter and experiences. And amidst the revelry, she couldn't shake the feeling of being exactly where she was meant to be, in a place where the ancient magic of the earth thrummed with life and possibility.

Meanwhile, Tiriaq observed the celebration from a distance with a mixture of surprise and intrigue. He had heard whispers of a visitor from the surface, a bearer of the Golden Lion, but he never imagined that he would encounter Ayuka so far from their home on the floating isle. As the crowd began to thin and the music faded into the night, he made his way through the village square, his heart pounding with anticipation at finally reuniting with his childhood friend.

As Tiriaq stood amidst the fading echoes of the celebration, he couldn't shake the surreal sight before him. The interplay between the two majestic creatures, the Shadow Lion and the Golden Lion, held him transfixed, their silent communication speaking volumes in the language of their kind. Each movement, each glance exchanged between them, seemed laden with significance, as if they shared a secret knowledge that transcended the boundaries of their earthly forms.

The Shadow Lion exuded an air of quiet intensity, its form wreathed in shadows that seemed to dance and flicker with a life of their own. Tiriaq felt a shiver run down his spine as he met its piercing gaze, sensing the weight of ancient wisdom and untold secrets hidden within its luminous eyes. Beside it, the Golden Lion radiated a warmth and light that seemed to pierce through the darkness, casting a golden glow that bathed the surrounding area in its ethereal luminescence.

Meanwhile, Ayuka caught up in the joy and camaraderie of the celebration, remained oblivious to the silent exchange between the two familiars. Her laughter echoed through the night air as she danced and mingled with the villagers, her carefree spirit a stark contrast to the solemnity of the moment. It was as if she had finally shed the weight of expectation and duty that had burdened her for so long, embracing the newfound freedom that came with being simply Ayuka, a young woman discovering her place in the world.

For Tiriaq, the sight was both mesmerizing and perplexing. He had grown up hearing tales of the bond between familiars and their chosen humans, but never had he witnessed such a profound interaction between two beings of such opposing natures. And yet, as he watched the Shadow Lion and the Golden Lion, he couldn't shake the feeling that their connection ran more profound than mere companionship, that they shared a bond forged in the crucible of destiny.

As the last strains of music faded into the night and the villagers began to disperse, Tiriaq took a tentative step forward, his heart pounding with excitement and apprehension. He knew he had to speak with Ayuka to unravel the mysteries that had brought them together in this unexpected reunion.

As the last remnants of the jubilant celebration dispersed, leaving behind an atmosphere tinged with lingering echoes of merriment, Tiriaq summoned his resolve to bridge the gap between himself and Ayuka. Each step felt heavy with the weight of anticipation, his heart hammering in his chest like a drum heralding an uncertain symphony. Around them, the village seemed to exhale a collective sigh of contentment, the flickering torches casting dancing shadows that mirrored the tumultuous emotions swirling within Tiriaq's soul.

Ayuka's gaze met his with astonishment and recognition, her eyes widening in surprise at his approach. Time seemed to stand still for a moment, suspended in the quiet space between them as they stood on the precipice of a long-awaited reunion. The flickering torchlight painted a mosaic of light and shadow across Ayuka's face, illuminating the delicate contours of her features and accentuating the warmth of her smile. In that fleeting moment, Tiriaq felt a surge of emotion welling within him, a potent blend of nostalgia and longing that threatened to overwhelm his senses.

With each step, Tiriaq closed the distance between himself and Ayuka, the air crackling with a palpable tension that seemed to hang suspended between them. He could feel the weight of their shared history pressing down upon him, a silent reminder of the bond that had once bound them together in childhood friendship. And as he finally stood before her, their eyes locked in a quiet exchange of understanding, Tiriaq felt a sense of clarity wash over him, as if the answers to the questions that had plagued him for so long were finally within his grasp.

Chapter 19: Rekindling

Ayuka's heart raced as she watched Tiriaq's steady stride toward her, his figure cutting through the crowd like a beacon of familiarity in the sea of unknown faces. Memories, long buried beneath the weight of time and distance, surged to the forefront of her mind, each a poignant reminder of their shared past. Her emotions swirled like leaves caught in a whirlwind—surprise at the unexpected reunion, confusion at the sudden flood of memories, and a hint of something deeper, something she couldn't quite name, tugging at the edges of her consciousness. His presence in Naji's village was a twist of fate she hadn't anticipated, a ripple in her carefully laid plans that threatened to unsettle the delicate balance she had worked so hard to maintain.

Tiriaq, too, was taken aback by the sight of Ayuka. Throughout his journey, her image had lingered in his thoughts like a beacon in the darkness, a constant reminder of the life he had left behind. He had often wondered how she fared in his absence, whether she still carried the weight of their shared past as heavily as he did. Now, seeing her standing before him, her expression a mixture of surprise and uncertainty, he felt a flood of conflicting emotions wash over him. Relief surged through his veins like a cool breeze on a sweltering day, knowing she was safe and sound. Yet, intertwined with that relief was a lingering apprehension, a gnawing fear of facing the consequences of their prolonged separation and the unresolved issues between them.

They stood silently for a moment, their eyes locked in a wordless exchange that spoke volumes. In that fleeting moment, it felt like time stood still, the world around them fading into insignificance as they grappled with the weight of their emotions. Then, tentatively, Ayuka broke the silence, her voice carrying a mixture of uncertainty and curiosity. "Tiriaq," she said, her tone soft yet filled with unspoken questions and emotions. The sound of his name, once so familiar yet now tinged with time, felt foreign and strangely comforting on her lips.

Tiriaq nodded in acknowledgment, his gaze softening as a small smile played at the corners of his lips. "Ayuka," he replied softly, his voice barely more than a whisper. In that fleeting moment, it felt like the years melted away, and they were once again the children they had been, their bond unbroken by the passage of time or the distance that had separated them. There was a familiarity in the way he spoke her name, a warmth that stirred memories long dormant within her heart.

As they began to speak, their words weaving a tapestry of shared experiences, Ayuka and Tiriaq found themselves effortlessly drawn into the rhythm of their conversation. Each sentence was like a brushstroke, painting vivid images of their childhood adventures on the floating Isle. They reminisced about the carefree days spent exploring hidden nooks and crannies, chasing after fleeting shadows, and marveling at the wonders of the natural world around them. Laughter bubbled up between them, a melodic symphony that echoed through the cavernous expanse of Naji's village, filling the air with a sense of warmth and camaraderie.

Their conversation meandered through the labyrinth of their memories, lingering on the bond they had forged with their familiars—the Golden Lion and the Shadow Lion. They recounted the day of their bonding ceremony, the anticipation that had thrummed in the air, and the awe-inspiring moment when they had first laid eyes on their destined companions. Ayuka spoke of the Golden Lion's radiant presence, its majestic form a beacon of light in the darkness. At the same time, Tiriaq shared tales of the Shadow Lion's enigmatic allure, its mysterious essence weaving through the fabric of their shared destiny.

Amidst their reminiscences, they also dared to broach the topic of their dreams for the future—dreams that had once burned bright with promise but had since been overshadowed by the weight of their responsibilities and the passage of time. They spoke of the aspirations they had harbored as children, the desires that had fueled their adventurous spirits and propelled them ever forward. And though their paths had diverged in unforeseen ways, leading them to separate corners of the world, they found solace in the realization that the essence of their dreams still lingered within them, waiting to be reignited.

As their conversation delved deeper into the recesses of their shared history, Ayuka and Tiriaq found themselves navigating through a labyrinth of emotions, where nostalgia intertwined with unease and fond memories collided with unresolved tensions. They spoke with candor about the circumstances that had led to their parting, the hurt and anger that had festered in the aftermath, and the lingering questions that had remained unanswered in their hearts.

With each word spoken, they peeled back the layers of their shared past, exposing raw emotions and unspoken truths that had long been buried beneath the surface. Ayuka spoke of the pain she had felt when Tiriaq had left the floating Isle, leaving behind a void that had seemed impossible to fill. She recounted the sleepless nights spent grappling with feelings of betrayal and abandonment; the tears shed in secret as she tried to make sense of the tumultuous whirlwind of emotions that had consumed her.

Tiriaq, in turn, bared his soul, revealing the guilt and regret that had weighed heavily on his conscience since their parting. He spoke of the internal conflict that had torn him apart between his duty to his family and his desire to forge his path in the world. He admitted to the pain he had caused Ayuka and the scars his absence had left on both their hearts, wounds that had yet to heal despite the passage of time fully.

As their conversation ventured into the depths of their shared history, Ayuka and Tiriaq found themselves navigating a maze of emotions. Nostalgia and sorrow intertwined as they revisited the events that had led to their parting, each word unraveling layers of unresolved tension and unspoken truths. Ayuka couldn't shake the lingering ache of Tiriaq's departure, a wound that had yet to heal despite the passing years fully. She spoke of the void his absence had left behind; the loneliness gnawed at her soul in the wake of his exile. With a heavy heart, she voiced the unfairness of it all, the weight of the burden he had been forced to bear for the sake of their former home. And yet, despite her understanding, a part of her couldn't help but question the circumstances that had torn them apart, the lingering "why" that echoed in the depths of her being, longing for an answer that may never come.

As they confronted the ghosts of their past, Ayuka and Tiriaq found themselves teetering on the precipice of vulnerability, their defenses crumbling in the face of their shared truth. They grappled with the complexities of their emotions, grappling with feelings of betrayal, anger, and heartache that threatened to engulf them.

And yet, amidst the pain and turmoil, they also discovered a glimmer of hope—a flickering ember of forgiveness and reconciliation that burned bright in the darkness, a beacon of light guiding them toward healing and renewal.

As the evening unfolded and the gentle glow of lanterns illuminated the village, Ayuka and Tiriaq found themselves enveloped in a cocoon of shared understanding and renewed hope. The weight of their past grievances began to lift, replaced by anticipation for the journey ahead. With each word exchanged and every lingering glance, they felt the tendrils of their connection weaving tighter, binding them together in a way that felt both familiar and new.

Under the canopy of stars that stretched across the night sky, Ayuka and Tiriaq stood on the brink of something transformative. It was a moment of clarity amidst the chaos of their past, a beacon of light illuminating the path forward. As they gazed into each other's eyes, they saw the reflection of their shared history and the promise of a future yet to be written.

Their hearts beat in unison, the rhythm of their bond echoing the silent promises exchanged between them. Yet, despite the newfound sense of connection, uncertainty lingered in the air like a whisper of the wind. They stood together, Ayuka with her Golden Lion by her side, Tiriaq with his Shadow Lion, their silhouettes outlined against the backdrop of the night sky.

In the quiet of the evening, surrounded by the gentle hum of the village and the distant calls of nocturnal creatures, they found themselves at a crossroads. The weight of their shared history hung heavy between them, a reminder of the challenges and hurdles still ahead. And as they stood there, bathed in the soft glow of moonlight, they couldn't help but wonder what the future held for them.

With a silent exchange, they turned to their familiars, seeking solace in the quiet companionship they offered. The Golden Lion and the Shadow Lion met their gazes with unwavering loyalty, their presence a source of strength and reassurance in the face of uncertainty.

Chapter 20: Destiny?

As Ayuka and Tiriaq nestled into the soothing aura of
their loyal lion companions, a shared understanding
settled between them; in the quiet intimacy of the
moment, they recognized the weight of unspoken
truths lingering between them, prompting a deep
yearning to bridge the gap that had grown during their
time apart. With a gentle nod from Ayuka, they began
to unravel the threads of their journeys, weaving
together a tapestry of experiences that painted a vivid
picture of the trials and revelations they had faced.

Sitting shoulder to shoulder, they delved into the
depths of their memories, each story a testament to the
resilience of the human spirit and the unyielding bond
between man and beast. Ayuka spoke first, her voice
soft yet filled with determination as she recounted the
whispers of the ancient forest and the echoes of
centuries-old tales that had stirred her soul. With each
word, she painted a vivid portrait of her encounters
with the forces of light and shadow, her eyes alight with
a fierce determination to protect the delicate balance of
the world.

Tiriaq listened intently, his gaze on Ayuka's face as she
spoke. He felt a pang of regret for their time apart, a
longing to reclaim their once-shared closeness. And yet,
as Ayuka's words washed over him, he felt a glimmer of

hope stir within his heart—a hope that perhaps their bond was not as fragile as he had feared.

As Ayuka's voice trailed off, Tiriaq took a deep breath, steeling himself to share his tale. Tiriaq's voice resonated with reverence and astonishment as he delved into his encounter with Naji and the profound revelations that had unfolded within the underground chamber. With each word, he painted a vivid picture of the mysteries that had captivated his mind and soul, his eyes alight with the intensity of his recollection.

He spoke of the enigmatic harbingers of a Beginning or an End, their presence casting a shadow over the world and stirring whispers of prophecy among those who dared to listen. He described The Goddess as a figure shrouded in myth and legend, whose influence seemed to permeate every corner of the land, guiding the destinies of mortals with an unseen hand.

But the vision had left the most profound impression on him—a kaleidoscope of light and shadow, a symphony of sound and silence that had transported him to the heart of the cosmos. He had glimpsed the golden lion in the depths of the swirling vortex, its majestic form radiant yet veiled in the shifting mists of uncertainty. And as its roar echoed through the chamber, he felt the weight of ancient knowledge wash over him, carrying the echoes of a long time.

As Tiriaq spoke, Ayuka listened with rapt attention, her eyes wide with wonder at the tales he wove. She could sense the magnitude of his experience and the depth of his connection to the mysteries hidden beneath the world's surface. And though she could not fully grasp the significance of his revelations, she felt a stirring within her soul—a recognition of the profound truths that resonated within his words and a newfound respect for the journey they had both taken.

As they delved deeper into their narratives, Ayuka and Tiriaq unearthed shared threads that wove through the tapestries of their journeys. They recounted the harrowing battles against the forces of shadow and celestial, the trials that tested their courage, and the sacrifices they willingly embraced in pursuit of a greater good. Each tale revealed layers of resilience and determination, echoing the other's struggles and triumphs in a symphony of shared experience.

As Ayuka and Tiriaq sat together, basking in the shared warmth of their newfound camaraderie, they couldn't shake the double-edged sword of hope that gripped their hearts. On one hand, there was a sense of optimism, a glimmer of possibility that danced on the horizon like a beacon in the night. The unexpected reunion had kindled a flame of hope within them, igniting dreams of reconciliation and a brighter future.

Yet, woven into their hope was a thread of apprehension, a silent acknowledgment of the uncertainties ahead. They knew all too well the perils that lurked in the shadows, the dangers that awaited those who dared challenge the status quo. Despite their shared resolve and determination, an unspoken fear whispered in their souls, casting a shadow over their newfound optimism.

As they exchanged fleeting glances and shared words of encouragement, Ayuka and Tiriaq grappled with the conflicting emotions tugging at their hearts. They felt the weight of responsibility pressing down on their shoulders, the burden of the journey they had embarked upon together. They couldn't help but wonder what the future held for them in the quiet moments between their conversations.

But amidst the swirling currents of hope and uncertainty, a quiet strength bound them together—a bond forged in the crucible of their shared experiences and tempered by their trials. They drew comfort from each other's presence, finding solace in knowing they were not alone in their struggles.

[The Tears]

"In the ethereal realm, the goddess weeps, her tears falling like shimmering stars upon the fractured world below. As cracks spiderweb across the once-stable fabric of reality, celestial forces rally with steely resolve, their luminous forms aglow with determination. They gather, their celestial armor gleaming, ready to wage war to destroy the encroaching darkness.

Meanwhile, in the depths of shadow, unseen and insidious, the forces of darkness scheme and plot. With twisted cunning, they weave illusions and sow seeds of discord among mortals, their malevolent whispers stirring unrest and turmoil.

As the celestial and shadow forces prepare for their inevitable clash, the world's fate hangs in the balance, teetering on the edge of oblivion. Amidst the chaos, the goddess's tears continue to fall, a silent lament for the fractured world she once knew.

Part 3: The Convergence

Chapter 21: To Sojourn

Ayuka and Tiriaq stood before Naji, their figures cast in flickering shadows by the soft glow of torchlight that lined the walls of the ancient chamber. The air seemed to hum with anticipation as if the very stones of the cavern were attuned to the moment's gravity. With his weathered face illuminated by the warm light, Naji exuded a quiet authority that commanded respect.

As he spoke, his voice resonated with the wisdom of ages past, each word carrying the weight of centuries of knowledge. "Your journey will not be easy," Naji began, his solemn tone filled with an undercurrent of reassurance. "But within you, both lies the light of hope and the strength of your bond." Deep and penetrating, his eyes met theirs with a silent understanding, conveying his unwavering belief in their abilities.

"You must trust in each other," Naji continued, his gaze unwavering, "for it is together that you will find the answers you seek." His words hung in the air, pregnant with meaning, as if he were imparting guidance and a sacred duty.

As they listened, Ayuka and Tiriaq felt a sense of reverence wash over them, their hearts swelling with a mixture of determination and trepidation. They knew that the journey ahead would test their courage and resilience like never before, but they also knew that they carried with them the blessings of Naji and the collective wisdom of the village.

With a solemn nod, they acknowledged Naji's words, their resolve strengthened by his unwavering faith in them. They were ready to embark on their quest, to face the challenges that awaited them with hearts open and spirits unyielding. And as they stepped out into the cool night air, guided by the light of the torches and the elder's wisdom, they knew that they carried with them the hopes and prayers of all people.

As they bid farewell to Naji and the villagers who had become their family, Ayuka and Tiriaq were enveloped in a bittersweet embrace of nostalgia and anticipation. Each goodbye felt like a weight upon their hearts, a reminder of the bonds they were leaving behind and the uncertain path ahead. Yet, amidst the sorrow of parting, there was also a flicker of excitement, a spark of determination that ignited their spirits.

The villagers gathered around them, their faces etched with expressions of both sadness and encouragement. They offered words of support and blessings, their voices mingling with the soft rustle of the evening breeze. Ayuka felt the comforting presence of the Golden Lion beside her, its radiant aura enveloping her in a sense of reassurance. Tiriaq, on the other hand, stood tall with the Shadow Lion by his side, its mysterious energy pulsating with silent strength.

With one last embrace and a final exchange of farewells, Ayuka and Tiriaq turned to face the open road before them. The night air was cool against their skin, carrying the scent of earth and adventure. Above, the stars twinkled brightly in the velvety sky, casting a celestial glow upon their journey.

Ayuka and Tiriaq's journey through the diverse landscapes was a kaleidoscope of encounters with different tribes, each offering a unique glimpse into the rich tapestry of the world they traversed. They met tribes nestled amidst verdant forests, their homes woven seamlessly into the lush foliage, and others dwelling in surprisingly warm dwellings amidst the cold, where torchlight danced against the walls adorned with ancient glyphs and symbols.

In their encounters with friendly tribes, Ayuka and Tiriaq were welcomed with open arms and embraced as honored guests among those who shared their hospitality. Sitting around crackling fires or beneath the cool shade of towering trees, they listened intently as tribal elders spun tales of ages past, recounting legends of the Goddess and her influence on the world. These stories, passed down through generations, held within

them kernels of wisdom and hidden truths, offering
Ayuka and Tiriaq valuable insights into the mysteries
they sought to unravel.

With each friendly encounter, Ayuka and Tiriaq
gathered not only knowledge but also allies, forging
bonds of friendship and mutual respect that would
bolster their spirits and lend strength to their quest. The
warmth of these connections provided solace amidst
their challenges, reminding them that they were not
alone in their journey and that the echoes of the
Goddess's legacy reverberated through the hearts of all
who sought to understand her mysteries.

As Ayuka and Tiriaq journeyed through the diverse
landscapes, they encountered tribes whose reception
was far from welcoming. Suspicion and hostility greeted
them in some places, with wary eyes following their
every move and weapons glinting in the sunlight as
warriors bristled with tension. Despite the imposing
presence of Tiriaq's Shadow Lion and Ayuka's Golden
Lion, these tribes remained steadfast in their distrust,
their demeanor a stark contrast to the warmth of the
friendly encounters.

For Ayuka and Tiriaq, these hostile encounters served as
sobering reminders of the precarious nature of their
quest. Despite the formidable strength at their side,
they found themselves navigating a delicate balance

between diplomacy and self-preservation. Every word spoken and step taken was fraught with tension as they sought to defuse the animosity and win over the hearts of those who suspected them.

Yet, amidst the threats and challenges, Ayuka and Tiriaq remained resolute, drawing upon the strength of their bond and the wisdom they had gained from their journey thus far. Whether friendly or hostile, each encounter served to steel their resolve and deepen their understanding of the world around them. And as they pressed onward, they knew they would need every ounce of determination and courage to overcome the obstacles ahead.

With weary yet determined steps, Ayuka and Tiriaq, accompanied by their faithful companions, the Golden Lion and the Shadow Lion, ascended the crest of a towering hill. The journey had been long and arduous, filled with trials and tribulations that tested their resolve at every turn. But as they reached the summit and beheld the breathtaking vista, a sense of fatigue and elation washed over them.

A lush green meadow was spread out below like a verdant tapestry, its vibrant hues starkly contrasting with the rugged terrain they had traversed. Beyond the meadow stretched the vast expanse of the ocean, its cerulean waters sparkling in the warm glow of the setting sun. And nestled amidst this idyllic scenery lay the village they had journeyed so far to find, its humble dwellings beckoning them from below.

For Ayuka and Tiriaq, the sight of the village brought joy and relief. It was a beacon of hope, a sanctuary where they hoped to find the answers they sought and the allies they needed to continue their quest. Despite the weariness that weighed heavily upon them, they felt a renewed sense of purpose stirring within their hearts as they descended toward the welcoming embrace of the village below.

Chapter 22: Unwelcome

As Tiriaq and the Shadow Lion, their forms silhouetted against the setting sun approached the outskirts of the village they had journeyed so far to find, they were met with an unexpected sight. Instead of the anticipated welcoming committee of villagers, the streets were eerily quiet, and the few people they glimpsed from afar hurriedly retreated indoors upon catching sight of them.

Tiriaq furrowed his brow in confusion, exchanging a bewildered glance with Ayuka as they advanced cautiously. The air crackled with tension, palpable even to the Shadow Lion, whose fur bristled in response to the charged atmosphere. Its golden eyes gleamed with apprehension and readiness, its instinctual senses on high alert.

Ayuka's grip on the Golden Lion's mane tightened subtly as she surveyed their surroundings, her heart sinking with each moment of silence. This was different from the warm reception they had anticipated. Instead, suspicion and hostility hung thick in the air, casting a shadow over their hopes of finding allies in the village.

The Shadow Lion emitted a low growl, its rumbling warning echoing through the deserted streets. It sensed the undercurrents of fear and mistrust that permeated the village, its instincts urging caution in the face of the unknown.

As they drew nearer to the heart of the village, Tiriaq and Ayuka exchanged concerned glances, silently steeling themselves for whatever awaited them beyond the looming shadows of uncertainty.

As Ayuka and Tiriaq, accompanied by their formidable lion companions, approached the outskirts of the village, the tension in the air became almost suffocating. Villagers, their faces etched with fear and mistrust, clustered together in small groups, casting wary glances toward the newcomers. Some hastily armed themselves with whatever makeshift weapons they could find, while others scurried to reinforce barricades hurriedly erected at the village's perimeter.

The atmosphere crackled with apprehension, the silence broken only by the murmurs of anxious voices and the faint rustle of leaves stirred by the evening breeze. Every step closer to the heart of the village felt like wading through a pool of trepidation, each movement laden with uncertainty.

The Shadow Lion's senses were keenly attuned to the escalating tension, its instincts honed by years of navigating the delicate balance between shadow and light. Its muscles tensed beneath its sleek coat, poised for action should the need arise. Beside it, the Golden Lion mirrored its companion's stance, its radiant form a stark contrast against the encroaching shadows. A low, rumbling growl emanated from deep within its chest, a warning to any who dared threaten its charge.

Ayuka and Tiriaq exchanged apprehensive glances, furrowing their brows with concern as they assessed the unfolding situation. The villagers' hostile demeanor was unexpected and unsettling, casting doubt on their hopes of finding allies in their quest. Yet, despite the palpable tension, they remained resolute, determined to defuse the situation and forge a path forward through diplomacy rather than conflict.

Despite the palpable tension thickening the air, Tiriaq and Ayuka stood firm in their resolve to quell the rising apprehension. Stepping forward with measured strides, they raised their hands in a gesture of goodwill, their voices projecting calm yet unwavering determination as they addressed the wary villagers gathered before them.

"Please, listen to us," Tiriaq's voice resonated across the quiet village square, each word carefully chosen to convey sincerity and reason. "We come not as adversaries but as seekers of knowledge and understanding. There is no need for conflict."

Beside him, Ayuka nodded in agreement, her gaze steady as it swept over the faces of the villagers. "We seek only peace and cooperation," she affirmed, her tone imbued with gentle reassurance. "Let us sit together and talk to dispel any misunderstandings and find common ground."

Their words hung like a fragile thread, poised delicately between tension and resolution. Still wary and uncertain, the villagers exchanged hesitant glances, their apprehension palpable. Yet, beneath the veneer of mistrust, a flicker of curiosity lingered, a seed of hope that perhaps, amidst the shadows of uncertainty, lay the possibility of reconciliation.

The weight of anticipation bore down upon them, every heartbeat echoing the tension that hung like a shroud over the village square. The villagers, their faces etched with fear and defiance, seemed poised on the brink of action, their collective gaze fixed unwaveringly on Tiriaq and Ayuka.

Feeling the moment's pressure mounting, Tiriaq's hand instinctively gripped his forehead in frustration. In a moment of reflexive impulse, a phrase from his youth passed down from his parents escaped his lips. "Tiaavuluk…" he muttered, the syllables falling from his lips like a forgotten incantation.

To his surprise, the effect was immediate. The tension in the air seemed to dissipate like morning mist beneath the sun's warming rays. The villagers, their expressions shifting from hostility to astonishment, paused in their preparations, their eyes widening in recognition.

Then, from the midst of the gathered crowd, a voice rang out, its tone tinged with disbelief and uncertainty. "Amaruq?" it whispered, the syllables carrying across the square like a gentle breeze through autumn leaves.

Tiriaq's plea echoed through the village square, his voice filled with desperation and sincerity. "Please! I am Tiriaq, Amaruq's son!" he implored, his words carrying the weight of generations of familial ties.

A palpable shift occurred among the villagers as his words hung in the air. Slowly, cautiously, suspicion began to yield to curiosity, and eyes that had once regarded him with mistrust now softened with tentative interest.

From the midst of the crowd, a figure emerged, shrouded in the folds of a weathered cloak. It was an older woman, her face etched with the lines of countless years, her gaze piercing as she regarded Tiriaq with a mix of scrutiny and recognition.

As the older woman stood in silence, her weathered features betraying no hint of her thoughts, a sense of unease settled over the gathering. Tiriaq could feel the weight of her scrutiny bearing down on him as if she were peering into the depths of his soul, searching for some truth hidden within.

In that charged moment, a subtle shift occurred in the atmosphere, almost imperceptible yet undeniable. Shadows seemed to lengthen, darkening the edges of the village square as if some unseen force were tightening its grip.

The Shadow Lion and the Golden Lion, attuned to the subtle fluctuations of energy around them, reacted instinctively. With a synchronized roar reverberating through the air like thunder, they sought to assert their presence, their voices intertwining in a primal display of power.

The villagers, taken aback by the sudden eruption of sound, recoiled instinctively, their eyes wide with a mixture of fear and awe. Some took a step back, casting wary glances at the majestic beasts before them, while others whispered among themselves, their voices hushed with uncertainty.

But to everyone's surprise, the older woman merely nodded, her gaze unwavering as she spoke. "Let them in," she declared, her voice carrying the weight of authority. And with her words, the tension that had gripped the village dissolved like morning mist beneath the rising sun.

Chapter 23: The Grey Wolf

In the flickering glow of the village fire, Tiriaq and Ayuka sat amidst the villagers, their faces illuminated by the dancing flames as they delved into the mysteries of Tiriaq's past. Initially met with guarded looks and whispered conversations, they soon found that patience and empathy opened doors that suspicion had firmly shut. Bit by bit, the villagers began to lower their defenses, their wariness giving way to a cautious curiosity.

Elders, their voices weathered with age and wisdom, spoke of a time when Amaruq, Tiriaq's father, was a revered community member. They painted a picture of a man of great integrity and honor, known for his deep connection to the land and its spirits. However, their voices grew somber when recounting the events leading to Amaruq's departure with a nomadic group, revealing the lingering uncertainty and unanswered questions that still haunted the village.

As the night wore on, Tiriaq and Ayuka listened intently, absorbing every detail and nuance of the stories shared with them. They learned of Amaruq's inexplicable departure, leaving behind a legacy shrouded in mystery and speculation. Yet, amidst the uncertainty, there was a reverence for the enigmatic figure, a recognition of his profound impact on the village and its people.

For Tiriaq, each revelation stirred a whirlwind of emotions within him—a longing to uncover the truth about his father's past, a sense of pride in the legacy he had inherited, and a determination to honor his memory by unraveling the mysteries surrounding him. Beside him, Ayuka offered silent support, her presence a steady anchor amid uncertainty as they navigated the complexities of Tiriaq's heritage together.

The fire crackled and popped, casting dancing shadows across the faces of those gathered around it. Tiriaq sat among them, his eyes fixed on the elders as they wove a tapestry of tales about his father, Amaruq. Each word spoken carried the weight of years gone by, imbued with a sense of reverence and mystery that hung heavy in the air.

The elders' voices, weathered by time and filled with the wisdom of generations, painted a vivid picture of Amaruq as a man of great integrity and honor. They spoke of his deep connection to the land and its spirits, his wisdom sought after by villagers far and wide. Yet, despite his esteemed reputation, Amaruq's sudden departure with a nomadic group had left the village reeling with unanswered questions and lingering uncertainty.

As the elders recounted the events leading to Amaruq's departure, Tiriaq felt a mixture of emotions stirring within him—curiosity, longing, and a profound sense of loss. He hung on every word, desperate to uncover the truth about his father's past and the legacy he had left behind. Beside him, Ayuka listened attentively, her presence a silent source of support as they delved deeper into the mysteries of Tiriaq's heritage.

As the fire's embers dimmed and the night stretched on, Tiriaq and Ayuka found themselves immersed in the villagers' tales, each revelation unveiling layers of suspicion and doubt. The villagers' skepticism toward the stories of The Goddess and The Island ran deep, rooted in generations of skepticism and wariness. They saw these tales not as sources of enlightenment but as tools of manipulation, crafted to maintain control and perpetuate false hope among the populace.

With furrowed brows and furled lips, the villagers spoke of The Island with disdain and apprehension. To them, it was not a bastion of safety but a mirage, a false paradise built on the shifting sands of deception. They warned Tiriaq and Ayuka of the dangers of trusting such myths, cautioning them against falling prey to the allure of false promises and empty dreams.

As Tiriaq and Ayuka listened, their hearts heavy with the weight of the villagers' distrust, they began to understand the depth of the divide between their beliefs and those of the villagers. The realization left them grappling with unease, their faith in The Island and its teachings shaken by the villagers' fervent convictions. Yet, amidst the discord, a glimmer of hope remained—a belief that somewhere, hidden within the shadows of doubt, lay the truth they sought.

Amid the villagers' skepticism and deep-seated mistrust, whispers circulated like wisps of smoke, hinting at a hidden truth veiled within the shadows of doubt. Among these murmurs, one tale stood out—a legend of a temple concealed within the labyrinthine depths of the wilderness, its existence known only to a select few and its location obscured by the passage of time.

According to the rumors that danced on the lips of the villagers, this temple held the key to unlocking the enigmatic secrets surrounding The Island and The Goddess. It was said to be guarded by ancient spirits, their ethereal forms weaving through the ancient stones like wisps of fog and shrouded in layers of protective enchantments designed to deter the unworthy and conceal its presence from prying eyes.

Yet, despite the veil of secrecy that cloaked its existence, tales of the temple persisted, passed down through generations like heirlooms of forbidden knowledge. For those who dared to venture into the wilderness in search of answers, the temple beckoned like a beacon of hope, its mysteries waiting to be unraveled by those brave enough to heed the call of adventure and uncover the truth hidden within its hallowed halls.

As the fire embers dwindled and the night grew darker, Tiriaq and Ayuka bathed in the soft glow of moonlight, casting elongated shadows that danced across the ground. Around them, the village slumbered, its inhabitants enveloped in the embrace of dreams, unaware of the momentous decision that hung in the air.

In the quiet of the night, Tiriaq and Ayuka exchanged knowing glances, a silent understanding passing between them like a gentle breeze rustling through the trees. Though their time in the village had been fraught with tension and uncertainty, it had also ignited a spark within them—a shared resolve to unearth the truth hidden within the depths of the wilderness.

With each revelation gleaned from the villagers' tales, their determination grew more assertive, fueled by a thirst for knowledge and answers that refused to be quenched. They knew that their journey was far from over and that the path ahead would be fraught with challenges and obstacles yet to be faced.

Feeling the chill of the night settle around them like a blanket, Tiriaq and Ayuka exchanged silent acknowledgments of their overstayed welcome. Yet, despite the villagers' waning hospitality, they found solace in each other's company, their bond a beacon of reassurance amidst the uncertainty surrounding them.

Bathed in the ethereal glow of the moonlight, they stood on the threshold of their next adventure, the silver beams casting long shadows that stretched out before them like whispers of fate. With each breath, they drew strength from the unspoken connection that bound them together; their resolve unwavering in the face of the unknown.

As they turned their gaze toward the looming wilderness, anticipation mingled with apprehension, the weight of their quest heavy upon their shoulders. Yet, with a shared sense of purpose guiding their footsteps, they stepped forward into the unknown, their hearts brimming with determination and their minds open to the possibilities ahead.

Through the dense undergrowth and towering trees, they pressed onward, the scent of pine and earth mingling in the air as if whispering secrets of the path ahead. Each step brought them closer to the heart of mystery and intrigue, their spirits undaunted by the challenges that awaited them on their journey into the unknown.

Chapter 24: The Temple

The dense foliage of the lush jungle enveloped Ayuka and Tiriaq like a verdant shroud as they ventured deeper into the wilderness, their senses heightened and attuned to every rustle and whisper in the undergrowth. The air hung heavy with humidity, suffusing the atmosphere with a palpable weight, while shafts of golden sunlight filtered through the canopy above, dappling the forest floor in shifting patterns of light and shadow. Amidst the tranquil beauty of their surroundings, an unspoken tension crackled in the air, an ominous undercurrent that whispered of the trials and tribulations that lay ahead on their journey. Every step forward seemed to bring them deeper into the heart of the unknown, each rustling leaf and fleeting shadow a reminder that they were not alone in this untamed realm.

As the celestial forces descended upon them with unexpected ferocity, Ayuka and Tiriaq found themselves thrust into a chaotic battle for survival. The Shadow Lion and the Golden Lion leaped into action beside them, their powerful forms moving with grace and precision as they met their adversaries head-on. Ayuka felt a surge of adrenaline coursing through her veins as she and the Shadow Lion fought as one, their movements fluid and coordinated. With each swipe of its claws and lunge of its robust frame, the Shadow Lion struck fear into the hearts of their foes, its shadowy form blending seamlessly with the darkness of the jungle.

Meanwhile, Tiriaq found himself locked in combat with the Golden Lion by his side, the creature's radiant presence imbuing him with a surge of magical energy that fueled his every move. Together, they fought with a surprising synergy, their bond manifesting in a dazzling display of coordinated attacks and strategic maneuvers. The magic of the Golden Lion lent Tiriaq a newfound strength and agility, enhancing his reflexes and imbuing his strikes with an otherworldly potency that left their enemies reeling.

As the battle raged on, Ayuka and Tiriaq found themselves drawing upon the unique strengths of their familiars and each other, their combined efforts driving back the celestial forces with unwavering determination. With each passing moment, their bond with their lions grew stronger, their unity in the face of adversity serving as a testament to the power of their shared purpose.

Despite the bruises and weariness that weighed heavily upon them, Ayuka and Tiriaq refused to falter in their quest, their resolve unshaken by the trials they had endured. With each step, they felt the pull of destiny, drawing them closer to their elusive goal, their hearts beating in rhythm with the pulse of the jungle around them.

Guided by an unseen force that seemed to beckon them forward, they ventured deeper into the heart of the dense foliage, their senses keenly attuned to the slightest signs of their surroundings. Amidst the towering trees and tangled vines, they stumbled upon the lost temple, its ancient stones bathed in dappled sunlight that filtered through the canopy above.

As they approached, a sense of reverence washed over them, their footsteps falling softly upon the moss-covered path leading to the temple's entrance. The air hummed with an aura of ancient power, the essence of the temple's presence permeating the surrounding jungle. With each passing moment, Ayuka and Tiriaq felt a growing sense of anticipation building within them, a palpable energy that crackled in the air like static before a storm.

Within the ancient chambers of the temple, Ayuka and Tiriaq's footsteps echoed against the weathered stone walls, their senses heightened by the weight of the revelation that hung heavy in the air. Illuminated by the soft glow of torchlight, they ventured deeper into the heart of the temple, guided by an instinctual pull toward the truth that lay hidden within its depths.

As Ayuka and Tiriaq ventured deeper into the heart of the temple, the walls whispered secrets of ages past through intricate carvings and cryptic inscriptions. Etched into the stone with painstaking precision, these ancient markings painted a vivid tapestry of the island's history, revealing the gradual waning of its once-potent magic.

The carvings' scenes were mesmerizing and ominous, showcasing the timeless conflict between celestial and shadowy forces. Celestial beings adorned with radiant wings clashed with their shadowy counterparts, their titanic struggle echoing through the annals of time. Each stroke of the chisel told a story of cosmic warfare, where the very fabric of reality hung in the balance.

Among the carvings, Ayuka and Tiriaq discerned the dire consequences of the island's fading magic. The world's delicate equilibrium teetered on the brink of collapse, threatened by the imbalance wrought by the diminishing magical energies. It was a cataclysmic scenario depicted in vivid detail, with the fate of entire civilizations hanging in the balance.

As they traced their fingers along the weathered inscriptions, Ayuka and Tiriaq felt the weight of their quest deepen. The revelations contained within the temple's walls painted a stark picture of the challenges ahead, igniting a fierce determination within them to restore the island's fading magic and avert the impending catastrophe foretold by the ancient carvings.

With each discovery, Ayuka and Tiriaq felt the weight of responsibility pressing upon them, their hearts heavy with the realization that the island's fate rested squarely on their shoulders. The appearance of the Shadow familiar only served to underscore the urgency of their quest, its presence a stark reminder of the impending doom that loomed on the horizon.

As they stood amidst the ancient ruins, bathed in the flickering light of torches, Ayuka and Tiriaq knew that they could not afford to falter in their mission. With determination burning bright in their hearts, they vowed to uncover a new source of magic to save the island from its inevitable demise and restore balance to the world again.

As Ayuka and Tiriaq deciphered the cryptic inscriptions adorning the temple walls, they unearthed the profound interconnectedness between the floating island and the surface world below. The ancient texts spoke of a symbiotic relationship forged eons ago, where the energies of the island and the surface intertwined to uphold the delicate balance of the universe.

Amidst the hallowed halls of the temple, Ayuka and Tiriaq immersed themselves in the depths of forgotten prophecies and enigmatic symbols, seeking to unravel the mysteries that lay shrouded in the mists of time. With each ancient scroll they unfurled and each cryptic symbol they deciphered, they gleaned a deeper understanding of the dire consequences that would befall both realms should the bond between the island and the surface be severed.

The prophecies spoke of a cosmic balance delicately maintained by the symbiotic relationship between celestial and shadowy forces. Through the reciprocal exchange of magic and energy, the realms remained in harmonious equilibrium, their intertwined fates woven into the very fabric of existence. However, should this bond be sundered, the consequences would be catastrophic.

The prophetic visions envisaged chaos and devastation, where cosmic forces clashed in a tumultuous struggle for dominance. Celestial realms fell into darkness, their radiant light snuffed out by the encroaching shadows, while the shadowy abyss consumed all in its path, leaving naught but desolation in its wake.

As Ayuka and Tiriaq pieced together the fragments of these ancient prophecies, a chilling realization dawned upon them. The fate of the island and the entire cosmos hung precariously in the balance. The bond between the realms was not merely a matter of survival for one world or the other but a fundamental aspect of cosmic harmony, with the potential to unleash untold destruction should it be disrupted.

As the weight of this revelation settled upon their shoulders, Ayuka and Tiriaq understood the gravity of their quest. They held the key to saving the island from its impending doom and bore the responsibility of preserving the very fabric of existence itself. With the stakes higher than ever, they vowed to harness their newfound knowledge and embark on a journey to restore the bond between the island and the surface, thus ensuring the survival of both realms for generations to come.

Chapter 25: Defiance

As Ayuka and Tiriaq sailed back to the floating Island, they couldn't shake the unease that seemed to hang like a heavy fog. The forces of celestial and shadow appeared to be growing stronger, their influence palpable as they neared their home. Dark clouds gathered ominously overhead, casting a shadow over the once serene waters, while eerie whispers carried on the wind, stirring the depths of their souls with a sense of foreboding.

Internally, both Ayuka and Tiriaq grappled with their doubts and fears. Despite their determination to save their home, uncertainty gnawed at their resolve, whispering doubts and planting seeds of discord in their minds. The weight of their responsibility pressed down on them like a heavy burden, threatening to crush their spirits beneath its crushing weight.

As Ayuka and Tiriaq, accompanied by the Golden Lion and Shadow Lion, reached the familiar desert at the base of the floating Island, they were met with trepidation and determination. The towering platform that served as the gateway to the Island loomed before them, its surface shimmering with an otherworldly glow as if infused with the very magic that sustained the floating landmass above.

As they approached the platform, the traditionalists who had gathered there resisted. Their expressions reflected a deep-seated reluctance to entertain the idea of challenging the Island's long-standing customs. The shadowy influence that seemed to cloud their judgment only exacerbated their fears and suspicions, creating a formidable barrier that threatened to derail Ayuka and Tiriaq's plans.

Undeterred, Ayuka and Tiriaq exchanged determined glances, silently communicating their resolve to press on despite the obstacles. With the Golden Lion and Shadow Lion by their side, they stepped forward, their voices ringing out with conviction as they attempted to sway the traditionalists to their cause.

"We understand your concerns, but the Island is in grave danger," Ayuka pleaded, her voice filled with urgency. "We need to find a new source of magic to sustain it, or else both the Island and the surface world will suffer."

Tiriaq's words echoed her sentiment, his tone firm yet earnest as he addressed the crowd. "We know this goes against everything you believe, but we cannot ignore the truth staring us in the face. Please, help us save our home."

Despite their impassioned pleas, the traditionalists remained unmoved, their resolve unshaken by the gravity of the situation. It seemed all hope was lost, and the platform remained stubbornly still, refusing to respond to their entreaties.

Despite their best efforts to reason with the traditionalists, Ayuka and Tiriaq met with closed minds and hardened hearts. The shadowy influence seemed to cloud their judgment, amplifying their fears and insecurities and driving them to cling ever tighter to the familiar comfort of tradition and routine.

As the tension reached its peak and despair threatened to overtake them, a low, ominous rumble echoed through the ground beneath their feet, causing the assembled crowd to fall silent in awe and wonder. The air crackled with anticipation as the platform, sensing the sincerity and determination of Ayuka and Tiriaq's cause, began to respond to their unwavering resolve.

At first, it was merely a subtle shift, a faint hum of energy vibrating through the air. Then, with a sudden burst of brilliance, the platform erupted in a dazzling display of light, its surface aglow with a soft, pulsating energy that seemed to pulse with the rhythm of their hearts.

With bated breath and wide-eyed wonder, Ayuka and Tiriaq watched in astonishment as the platform responded to their presence, its once-inert surface shimmering with newfound vitality. It began to rise slowly but steadily, defying gravity as it carried them upward toward the floating Island above.

As they ascended higher and higher into the sky, the world around them seemed to blur into a kaleidoscope of colors and sensations. The wind whispered secrets of ancient magic while the stars above twinkled with silent approval.

Chapter 26: Returning and Revelation

As Ayuka and Tiriaq set foot on the lush, verdant ground of the Floating Island, a sense of foreboding gripped them, contrasting sharply with the fond memories of homecoming they had anticipated. The once-familiar sights and sounds of their island paradise seemed tinged with an eerie stillness, as if an unseen force had muted the very essence of the place. Faces they had known since childhood, usually beaming with warmth and welcome, now regarded them with guarded expressions, their eyes betraying suspicion and concern. Even their families, who had always been their steadfast supporters, now stood at a distance, their arms crossed and brows furrowed with unease. It was as though a shadow had been cast over the island, shrouding it in a thick cloak of doubt and apprehension, leaving Ayuka and Tiriaq to navigate the unsettling atmosphere with a heavy heart.

Once a source of comfort and familiarity, the lush, verdant ground beneath their feet now seemed to hold an air of secrecy and uncertainty. The vibrant hues of the flora that once adorned the landscape now appeared muted, as if drained of their vitality by the pervasive foreboding in the air. The soft rustle of leaves and the gentle chirping of birds, once the soothing soundtrack of their island home, now felt almost ominous, as if carrying whispers of secrets untold and truths yet to be revealed.

Every familiar face they encountered seemed to harbor hidden depths of doubt and suspicion, their smiles strained and their greetings lacking the warmth that had once defined their interactions. Friends who had once shared laughter and camaraderie now regarded them with a wary gaze, their expressions clouded by unspoken questions and unvoiced concerns. It was as though a veil had been drawn over their shared history, obscuring the bonds of friendship and trust that had once bound them together.

As Ayuka and Tiriaq made their way through the once-bustling streets of the Floating Island, they couldn't shake the feeling of being intruders in their own homes. The air seemed to hum with tension as if the island held its breath, waiting for some unseen event to unfold. Even the buildings and landmarks that had once stood as symbols of their resilience and unity now seemed to loom ominously overhead, casting long shadows that stretched across the landscape like dark fingers reaching out to grasp them.

Their families, usually the anchors that grounded them amidst life's storms, now stood aloof and distant, their expressions unreadable as they watched Ayuka and Tiriaq's every move with a mixture of curiosity and apprehension. It starkly contrasted the warm embraces and words of encouragement that had greeted them in the past, leaving Ayuka and Tiriaq feeling adrift in a sea of uncertainty and doubt.

The villagers once unified in their customs and beliefs, now seemed divided in their reception of Ayuka and Tiriaq. Some, swayed by the whispers of shadowy forces that lingered in the air, viewed the duo with suspicion and mistrust, eager to maintain the status quo and resist any disruption to their way of life. Others, perhaps more open-minded or less influenced by external forces, remained cautiously curious, willing to hear what Ayuka and Tiriaq had to say before passing judgment.

As Ayuka and Tiriaq attempted to navigate their community's intricate social dynamics, they faced many challenges, each designed to test their resolve and determination. Some villagers, emboldened by the lingering shadows that seemed to cling to their hearts, sought to undermine their efforts at every turn, sowing seeds of doubt and discord wherever they went. Others, more sympathetic to their cause, offered quiet words of encouragement and support, their gestures of solidarity a beacon of hope amidst the growing darkness.

Despite their best efforts to remain united, Ayuka and Tiriaq soon found themselves isolated and alone, each one forced to navigate the treacherous waters of their home island's politics without the support of their friends and family. The once-strong bonds of camaraderie and kinship that had defined their community now seemed fragile and tenuous, stretched to their breaking point by suspicion and mistrust.

Separated by the invisible barriers that now divided their village, Ayuka and Tiriaq struggled to find common ground amidst the growing discord. Each one faced unique challenges and obstacles; they found themselves increasingly isolated from one another, their shared journey threatened by the very forces they had hoped to overcome.

As Tiriaq and the Shadow Lion ventured deeper into the heart of the island, they encountered a series of mystical barriers, unlike anything they had ever faced before. These barriers, woven from ancient magic and reinforced by centuries of tradition, seemed impervious to their usual escape methods. No matter how hard they tried to break through, their physical strength proved futile against the insidious enchantments that held them captive.

With each passing moment, the sense of urgency grew, the weight of their predicament bearing upon them like a suffocating blanket. The Shadow Lion, usually a formidable companion in times of need, seemed equally frustrated by their inability to overcome the magical barriers surrounding them, its golden eyes blazing with determination and desperation.

As they searched for a way out, Tiriaq and the Shadow Lion found themselves confronted by a maze of twisting corridors and hidden passageways, each more treacherous than the last. The air crackled with latent energy, the faint hum of magic echoing through the stone walls as they pressed on, their senses heightened by the ever-present threat of danger.

Despite their efforts to remain calm and focused, the oppressive atmosphere weighed heavily upon them, sapping their strength and testing their resolve. With each failed attempt to find an exit, the hopelessness threatened to consume them, their spirits dampened by the relentless onslaught of obstacles that stood in their way.

As Ayuka and the Golden Lion embarked on their trials, they found themselves confronted with a series of daunting challenges that tested not only their physical prowess but also their mental fortitude. Each task seemed more formidable than the last, pushing them to their limits and beyond as they struggled to prove themselves worthy in the eyes of Ayuka's father, the island's leader.

Ayuka and the Golden Lion faced seemingly insurmountable odds with each new challenge, their magical abilities providing little assistance in the face of the physical tests that lay ahead. They battled through dense jungles teeming with hostile wildlife, scaled towering cliffs slick with rain and mist, and traversed treacherous ravines that threatened to swallow them whole.

Despite their best efforts, they found themselves outmatched at every turn, their usual strengths rendered useless against the unforgiving terrain and relentless adversaries that barred their path. Ayuka's father, watching from a distance, seemed unmoved by their struggles, his expression a mask of stoicism as he observed their every move with keen interest.

As the trials wore on, Ayuka and the Golden Lion felt the weight of their failures pressing down upon them, the impending doom looming ever closer with each passing moment. Yet, despite the overwhelming odds stacked against them, they refused to give up, drawing strength from their unwavering determination and the unbreakable bond that bound them together.

As tension peaked and despair threatened to consume them, a palpable shift occurred in the atmosphere surrounding Ayuka and Tiriaq. It was as if the air hummed with an otherworldly energy, crackling with an intensity that seemed to defy comprehension. At that moment, the laws of nature appeared to bend and warp as though responding to the presence of some ancient, long-forgotten magic.

Then, with a sudden and awe-inspiring burst of light, the truth they sought was revealed in a dazzling display of power. The once-shrouded identities of their loyal companions, the Shadow Lion, and the Golden Lion, were laid bare before them. It was a revelation that defied all logic and reason, yet there could be no denying the undeniable truth that stood before them.

As the radiant glow faded, replaced by a serene calmness that seemed to settle over the group, Ayuka and Tiriaq found themselves gazing upon their companions with newfound clarity. The Shadow Lion, once cloaked in darkness and mystery, now shone with a radiant golden light, its form transformed into that of the revered Golden Lion. Conversely, the Golden Lion, once a beacon of celestial magic, now stood before them as the enigmatic Shadow Lion, its presence imbued with a darkness that belied its true nature.

In the wake of this profound revelation, a sense of awe and wonder washed over Ayuka and Tiriaq, their minds struggling to comprehend the magnitude of what had just occurred. It was as though the very fabric of reality had shifted, revealing a truth that had long been hidden from view.

With their faithful familiars revealed, a surge of confidence and newfound strength coursed through Ayuka and Tiriaq. No longer bound by the limitations imposed by their false identities, they found themselves imbued with a sense of clarity and purpose that propelled them forward with unwavering resolve.

For Tiriaq, the transformation was nothing short of miraculous. With the Golden Lion by his side, he felt a surge of power and confidence, unlike anything he had ever experienced. The once-daunting labyrinth that had ensnared him now seemed like a mere playground, its intricate twists and turns navigated easily as he and his loyal companion pressed onward.

Meanwhile, Ayuka felt profound liberation as she embraced her true identity alongside the Shadow Lion. No longer constrained by the expectations placed upon her, she felt a newfound strength and resilience coursing through her veins. Each obstacle they encountered was met with unwavering determination, her connection with her companion guiding her with steadfast clarity.

Separated within the labyrinth, Tiriaq found himself navigating the intricate passages with newfound ease, empowered by the revelation of his true familiar, the Golden Lion. With each step, he felt a surge of confidence coursing through him, his connection to the ancient magic of the island guiding him effortlessly through the maze of enchanted traps and barriers.

Meanwhile, Ayuka faced daunting challenges that tested her physical strength and resilience. Tasked with feats of strength beyond her usual capabilities, she summoned every ounce of determination and resolve within her. Her bond with the Shadow Lion infused her with a newfound power and purpose. Despite the formidable obstacles before her, she pressed on with unwavering determination, driven by the knowledge that the fate of their world depended on her success.

As Tiriaq delved deeper into the labyrinth, he uncovered ancient symbols and cryptic inscriptions that hinted at the existence of a sacred place at the heart of the island. Guided by the wisdom of his newfound familiar, he pieced together the clues scattered throughout the maze, each revelation bringing him closer to unlocking the secrets hidden within the island's core.

Meanwhile, Ayuka faced increasingly difficult trials that pushed her to her limits, each victory bringing her one step closer to unlocking her true potential. With each challenge she overcame, she felt the strength of her bond with the Shadow Lion growing more substantial, the ancient magic of their connection imbuing her with an unshakeable sense of confidence and determination.

Having triumphed over the final trial, Ayuka stood before her father, the island's leader, her chest heaving with exertion and her brow furrowed with determination. As she met his gaze, the Shadow Lion at her side let out a mighty roar, its form pulsating with ancient power as it unleashed a wave of energy that dispersed the shadows that seemed to cling to her father.

With a solemn nod, Ayuka's father expressed his gratitude, his eyes reflecting pride and admiration as he embraced her tightly. They momentarily stood locked in a heartfelt embrace, the weight of their shared journey hanging heavy in the air. But as he pulled away, a sudden sense of alarm flashed across his face, and he shook his head as if to clear his thoughts. Urgency replaced sentimentality as he hurried Ayuka along, urging her to make haste to the sacred place at the heart of the island. There, the fate of their world awaited, and there was no time to waste. With a determined nod, Ayuka set off, her resolve strengthened by her father's words and the knowledge that the future hung in the balance.

[The Light]

In the heart of the celestial realm, where time and space melded into a dance of light and energy, a gathering of celestial beings took place. Among them stood The Guardian, a shimmering being of pure light, her presence commanding the attention of all who surrounded her. She was The Guardian of the Celestial Realm, tasked with maintaining the delicate balance that held the cosmos together.

As the celestial beings convened, a sense of unease permeated the air. It was rare for such a meeting to be called, and the gravity of the situation was evident in the solemn expressions that adorned the faces of those gathered.

At the forefront of the assembly stood The Guardian, her luminous form radiating with an otherworldly glow. Beside her stood The Sage, the ancient sage of the stars, his eyes filled with a wisdom that transcended time.

"Guardian," The Sage spoke, his voice echoing through the celestial chamber, "the balance of the cosmos is under threat. A darkness looms on the horizon, threatening to engulf all we hold dear."

The Guardian's brow furrowed with concern as she listened to The Sage's words. She had sensed the disturbance in the fabric of reality, but she had hoped it was merely a fleeting shadow in the vast expanse of the cosmos.

"What do you propose we do, Sage?" The Guardian asked, her voice tinged with a hint of apprehension.

"We must act swiftly," The Sage replied, his gaze unwavering. "We must gather our forces and destroy the darkness before it can spread further."

And so, with a sense of purpose burning in their hearts, the celestial beings rallied together, their collective light shining brightly against the encroaching darkness. For they knew that the fate of the cosmos hung in the balance, and only by standing united could they hope to prevail against the forces of darkness.

[The Shadow]

In the depths of the astral plane, where shadows danced, and darkness held sway, a gathering of shadowy figures took place. These enigmatic beings, shrouded in obscurity and cloaked in mystery, convened in the dimly lit chambers of the void.

At the forefront of the assembly stood The Master, a towering figure wreathed in darkness, commanding the respect of all who surrounded him. He was the Master of Shadows, ruler of the dark realm, and his eyes burned with a malevolent gleam as he addressed his assembled minions.

"Fellow shadows," The Master's voice echoed through the chamber, sending shivers down the spines of those gathered. "The time has come to unleash our darkness upon the mortal realm. The time has come to assert our dominance over the forces of light."

The shadowy figures murmured their agreement, their voices barely more than whispers in the darkness. They hungered for power and sought to spread their influence across the realms, bending reality to their will.

"But first," The Master continued, his voice dripping with malice, "we must deal with those who would oppose us. The forces of light gather their strength, and we must strike swiftly and decisively if we are to emerge victorious."

With a sense of purpose burning in their hearts, the shadowy figures pledged their allegiance to The Master, their loyalty unwavering as they prepared to unleash their darkness upon the mortal realm. For they knew that the fate of the astral plane hung in the balance, and only by standing united could they hope to overcome the forces of light and emerge triumphant.

Chapter 27: Conflict

In the heart of the Island, amidst the ethereal crystal glow and the whispering winds, Tiriaq and the Golden Lion found themselves drawn inexplicably closer to Ayuka and the Shadow Lion. As they emerged from the ethereal rock, the sight of their companions waiting for them filled them with relief and wonder.

Tiriaq and the Golden Lion approached with hesitant steps, their hearts pounding with anticipation. Ayuka and the Shadow Lion stood before them, their eyes reflecting the flickering light filtering through the canopy above. Time seemed to stand still for a moment as they closed the distance between them, the air electric with the palpable energy of their reunion.

Then, in a rush of emotion, they embraced, the warmth of their companions' presence washing over them like a soothing balm. It was a moment of profound connection, a reaffirmation of the unbreakable bond that had brought them together in the first place. As they held each other tightly, the weight of their shared experiences seemed to lift, replaced by a sense of unity and purpose.

In that fleeting moment, they were not just individuals embarking on a perilous journey but a team bound by friendship, trust, and a shared destiny. And as they stood together, their spirits intertwined like the roots of an ancient tree, they knew that no matter what trials lay ahead, they would face them united, drawing strength from each other every step of the way.

As they stood together in the heart of the Island, surrounded by the gentle rustle of leaves and the soft glow of sunlight filtering through the canopy above, Tiriaq and Ayuka exchanged bewildered glances. The transformation of their familiars hung heavy in the air, casting a shadow over their reunion.

With furrowed brows and furled lips, they struggled to make sense of the sudden change. The Golden Lion, once a symbol of celestial strength and purity, now bore the markings of shadow, its fur tinged with darkness that seemed to swirl and shift like smoke. Similarly, the Shadow Lion, once a harbinger of darkness and mystery, now emanated a soft golden light, its eyes gleaming with an otherworldly radiance.

Questions tumbled through their minds like stones in a rushing river, each more perplexing than the last. What force had wrought this transformation upon their familiars, and what did it signify for their quest to restore balance to the Island? Could it be that their companions held secrets far more profound than they had ever imagined, secrets that could hold the key to unlocking the mysteries of their world?

With furrowed brows and furled lips, they struggled to make sense of the sudden change. The Golden Lion, once a symbol of celestial strength and purity, now bore the markings of shadow, its fur tinged with darkness that seemed to swirl and shift like smoke. Similarly, the Shadow Lion, once a harbinger of darkness and mystery, now emanated a soft golden light, its eyes gleaming with an otherworldly radiance.

Questions tumbled through their minds like stones in a rushing river, each more perplexing than the last. What force had wrought this transformation upon their familiars, and what did it signify for their quest to restore balance to the Island? Could it be that their companions held secrets far more profound than they had ever imagined, secrets that could hold the key to unlocking the mysteries of their world?

However, before they could unravel the enigma, a deafening roar shattered the tranquility, signaling the convergence of the forces of shadow and celestial. The ground beneath their feet quivered with the weight of impending doom while the air crackled with the energy of impending conflict.

In the distance, the clash of darkness and light erupted like a symphony of chaos, each thunderous boom reverberating through the very core of the Island. Shadows danced with ethereal light, locked in a fierce struggle for dominance as the celestial and shadowy forces clashed with unimaginable ferocity.

Tiriaq and Ayuka exchanged urgent glances, their hearts pounding in their chests as they realized the gravity of the situation. This was no mere skirmish; it was a battle for the very fate of their world, a clash of opposing powers that threatened to consume everything in its path.

With resolve hardening in their hearts, they knew they could not stand idly by while their world crumbled around them. As one, they braced themselves for the coming storm, ready to face whatever challenges lay ahead to restore balance and save their home from oblivion.

Chapter 28: The Clash of Light and Shadow

As Tiriaq, the Golden Lion, and Ayuka with the Shadow Lion reached the heart of the Island, they were greeted by a spectacle unlike any they had ever witnessed. Before them, the forces of Light and Shadow clashed ferociously, each side locked in a desperate struggle for dominance.

Amidst the celestial beings, two figures emerged as prominent leaders of the Light forces: The Guardian and The Sage. The Guardian, towering and imposing, radiated an aura of unwavering strength and determination. Clad in armor that gleamed with divine light, they brandished a mighty sword, embodying their commitment to protecting the celestial realm from all threats, perceived or otherwise.

Beside The Guardian stood The Sage, a figure of wisdom and insight, their presence commanding the respect of all who beheld them. With eyes that seemed to pierce the very fabric of reality, The Sage wielded knowledge as their most potent weapon, guiding the celestial forces with sagacious counsel and strategic brilliance.

Together, The Guardian and The Sage led the charge against the forces of Shadow, their righteous fervor unyielding as they sought to purge the celestial realm of darkness once and for all. With each swing of The Guardian's sword and each word of wisdom from The Sage's lips, they inspired their comrades to fight with unwavering resolve, confident in the righteousness of their cause.

The Guardian and The Sage pressed on, leading their forces with unwavering determination as they sought to vanquish the darkness. For them, there could be no compromise, no hesitation—not when the fate of the celestial realm hung in the balance.

At the forefront of the shadowy forces stood The Master, a figure shrouded in darkness and draped in mystery. With an air of calculated menace, The Master exuded an aura of cunning and ruthlessness, their every move a testament to their mastery of manipulation and deceit. Cloaked in shadows that seemed to writhe and twist around them like living tendrils, they commanded their minions with icy precision, orchestrating their every move with meticulous planning and forethought.

With a flick of their hand, The Master unleashed waves of darkness across the battlefield, enveloping their enemies in a suffocating shroud of despair. Their strategy was one of subterfuge and misdirection, sowing chaos and confusion amongst the ranks of the celestial forces as they sought to exploit every weakness and vulnerability.

As The Master surveyed the chaos they had wrought, a twisted smile played across their lips, their eyes gleaming with cruel satisfaction. To them, the clash between Light and Shadow was not merely a battle for dominance but a grand spectacle, a theater of cruelty and suffering in which they reveled with perverse delight.

And so, as the clash between Light and Shadow raged on, The Master remained vigilant, their mind sharp and their senses honed as they sought to outmaneuver their foes at every turn. In the cosmic dance of power and intrigue, only the cunning and the ruthless would emerge victorious, and The Master intended to be among them.

As Tiriaq, Ayuka, and their loyal companions bore witness to the epic clash between the forces of Light and Shadow, they were caught in a maelstrom of chaos and power unlike anything they had ever experienced. Each thunderous clash reverberated through the air, sending shockwaves rippling across the battlefield, while celestial and shadowy energy arcs illuminated the sky with otherworldly brilliance.

Caught between the celestial beings and the shadowy figures, Tiriaq and Ayuka felt the moment's weight pressing down upon them like a heavy cloak. Their hearts pounded in their chests as they watched the forces of Light and Shadow lock horns in a battle for supremacy, knowing that the outcome would shape the destiny of their world for eons to come.

Despite the awe-inspiring spectacle unfolding before them, Tiriaq and Ayuka felt a sense of shock and disbelief as they struggled to comprehend the magnitude of the conflict. It was as if the very fabric of reality itself was being torn asunder before their eyes, and they could do nothing but stand in silent awe of the forces at play.

Amid the chaos, they could feel the ground trembling beneath their feet with each thunderous impact, the sheer force of the battle threatening to engulf them. Yet amidst the turmoil and destruction, a glimmer of determination burned bright in their hearts, driving them forward to restore balance to their world.

As they stood on the precipice of destiny, Tiriaq and Ayuka knew that they must tread carefully to navigate the treacherous waters of this conflict. For in the crucible of war, alliances were forged and loyalties tested, and they could ill afford to make a misstep in their quest to save their world from oblivion.

Chapter 29: A Chance

Amidst the tumultuous clash between the forces of Light and Shadow, Tiriaq and Ayuka found themselves inexplicably drawn towards a serene oasis of tranquility amidst the chaos. It was as if the very fabric of reality had shifted to accommodate their presence, offering them respite from the relentless storm around them.

The Lions were drawn Into a dance by the primal forces that guided them, the cosmic energies that pulsed through their very beings. As Tiriaq and Ayuka stepped into the heart of the pocket of stillness, a convergence of celestial and shadowy energies surrounded them, suffusing the air with a palpable tension. Sensing the need for balance amidst the chaos of the battlefield, the Golden Lion and Shadow Lion instinctively moved towards each other, their movements mirroring the intricate dance of the universe itself.

With each graceful step, they communicated wordlessly, their intentions clear, and their purpose unified. It was as if the very essence of their existence compelled them to come together, to bridge the gap between light and shadow, order and chaos. As they circled each other in a mesmerizing display of divine choreography, the energies around them swirled and surged, building towards a crescendo of cosmic significance.

In that moment, the Lions became conduits for the universal forces at play, channeling the divine energies that flowed through them gracefully and precisely. Their dance was not just a physical movement but a spiritual communion, a sacred ritual that transcended the boundaries of time and space. And as they moved in perfect harmony, their fusion seemed inevitable, a manifestation of the cosmic balance sought amidst the battlefield's turmoil.

As they drew nearer, the boundary between them began to blur, their distinct forms melding together in a breathtaking display of divine alchemy. The Golden Lion's mane shimmered with iridescent hues of gold and silver, while the Shadow Lion's fur seemed to ripple with an ever-changing array of shades and tones.

The fusion reached its climax in a radiant burst of celestial light, and Tiriaq and Ayuka watched in awe as the Golden Lion and Shadow Lion became one. Their merged form radiated a transcendent glow, embodying the perfect balance of Light and Shadow, strength and grace. It was a sight to behold, a testament to the power of unity and harmony in the face of chaos and discord.

With the fusion complete, a profound sense of peace washed over Tiriaq and Ayuka, filling their hearts with renewed purpose and resolve. As they gazed upon the radiant form of the merged lion, they knew they had witnessed something extraordinary—a divine union born from their courage and conviction.

In the heart of the battlefield, where the clash of celestial and shadowy forces raged, the Lion of divine balance emerged as a beacon of tranquility amidst the chaos. Its majestic form glowed with a radiant light, illuminating the surrounding darkness with a mesmerizing aura that seemed to transcend the boundaries of the mortal realm.

As the Lion moved with unparalleled grace and fluidity, its movements reminiscent of a celestial dance, it exuded an otherworldly presence that commanded awe and reverence. With each step, it left behind a shimmering energy trail weaving a tapestry of celestial and shadowy hues that danced and intertwined in a mesmerizing display of harmony.

The celestial forces, accustomed to the blinding brilliance of their light, found themselves disarmed by the ethereal radiance of the divine Lion. Its presence seemed to soothe their fervor, calming the tumultuous energies that had fueled their relentless onslaught.

Similarly, the shadowy forces, shrouded in darkness and mystery, were entranced by the Lion's soothing aura. As it moved among them, its gentle touch seemed to quell the restless shadows, bringing peace to the chaotic battlefield.

Amidst the swirling energies of light and shadow, the Lion of divine balance symbolized unity and equilibrium, bridging the divide between opposing forces with its transcendent presence. As it moved with unparalleled grace and serenity, it brought a moment of respite to the weary combatants, offering a glimpse of hope amidst the turmoil of war.

As the Lion approached the clash between The Master and The Guardian, with The Sage nearby assisting the Guardian, a hush fell over the battlefield. The celestial and shadowy forces paused in their relentless combat, their attention drawn to the mesmerizing spectacle unfolding before them.

In a moment of eerie silence, The Master and The Guardian locked eyes, their expressions a mixture of surprise and curiosity. The Sage, standing steadfast beside the Guardian, raised a hand in a gesture of caution, his wise eyes reflecting the moment's uncertainty.

Then, as if guided by an unseen force, their gazes turned towards Tiriaq and Ayuka, the chosen champions who had unwittingly brought about this divine intervention. There was a palpable tension in the air as they stared at the two mortals, their fates intertwined with the cosmic forces at play.

Chapter 30

"Tiriaq," Ayuka began, her voice barely a whisper amidst the cacophony of battle yet carrying a weight of profound introspection, "do you ever find yourself grappling with the duality of our existence?" Her words hung in the air, a delicate thread woven between them, drawing Tiriaq's attention away from the tumultuous clash of celestial and shadowy forces around them.

Tiriaq furrowed his brow, his gaze drifting from the radiant bursts of light to the murky depths of darkness that danced on the fringes of their reality. "Yes, Ayuka," he replied after a moment, his voice tinged with a hint of vulnerability, "I do. It's like a constant tug-of-war, a battle between the light and shadow in my heart."

Ayuka nodded in understanding, her eyes reflecting the turmoil mirrored within Tiriaq's soul. "I know what you mean," she murmured, her voice a gentle echo of empathy. "There are times when I feel the pull of darkness, its seductive whispers tempting me to stray from the path of righteousness. But then, there are moments of clarity when the light within me shines through, guiding me back to the path of truth and virtue."

Tiriaq listened intently, his heart heavy with their shared struggle. "It's a constant battle," he admitted, his voice tinged with resignation and determination.

They stared at the figures, staring back at them, at an impasse. The world hung in the balance, and the Harbingers were lost in introspective thought.

Tiriaq's gaze swept over the gathered figures, each embodying a different aspect of the cosmic balance. His voice, tinged with resignation and frustration, echoed in the air, carrying the weight of his inner turmoil. The memory of his exile loomed large in his mind, a constant reminder of the upheaval and uncertainty that had defined his journey thus far.

As he looked at Ayuka, the Divine Lion, he couldn't help but feel a twinge of envy for her unwavering sense of purpose and clarity. She stood before him, a beacon of strength and wisdom, radiating an aura of divine grace that seemed to illuminate the darkness around them.

The celestial figures, their luminous forms shimmering with ethereal light, regarded Tiriaq with compassion and curiosity. They understood his struggles and the inner conflict that threatened to consume him, and they waited patiently for his words, knowing that sometimes speaking aloud one's doubts and fears could be a step towards finding clarity and resolution.

Tiriaq voiced his innermost thoughts with a heavy sigh, laying bare the uncertainty that plagued him. His words hung in the air, a poignant expression of his longing for answers in a world fraught with ambiguity and complexity. He wondered aloud if the absence of a definitive answer was a form of liberation, a pathway to self-discovery and enlightenment.

Tiriaq looked at Ayuka, The Divine Lion, and the celestial figures and sighed aloud, "Ever since my Exile, I've been drifting along, having no choice in what I do or where I go. This feels like a long shot, but is having no answer the answer?"

The Divine beings stared at them, clearly not.

Tiriaq's words resonated with a raw honesty, each syllable carrying the weight of his tumultuous journey. He spoke of exile, uncertainty, and being adrift in a sea of fate without a compass to guide him. His lament echoed through the chamber, a poignant reminder of the fragility of their existence in a world governed by forces beyond their control.

As Ayuka listened to Tiriaq's lament, a surge of empathy welled within her. She understood the weight of his burden, the crushing weight of uncertainty that threatened to engulf him. With a silent nod of understanding, she stepped forward, her presence a beacon of strength and reassurance amidst the swirling chaos.

With a deep breath, Ayuka stepped forward, her gaze steady and resolute as she addressed the celestial figures before them. "Perhaps," she began, her voice ringing out with a quiet strength, "the absence of an answer is not a failure but an invitation to embrace the uncertainty of our journey." The divine beings regarded her words with curiosity and skepticism, their luminous forms shimmering with an otherworldly glow. But Ayuka, channeling the wisdom of the Golden Lion, saw beyond the confines of fate, recognizing the inherent beauty in the unpredictability of existence. "In the absence of certainty," she continued, her voice echoing with conviction, "lies the freedom to forge our path, to chart a course guided by our hopes, dreams, and desires."

Her words hung in the air, challenging the celestial beings to reconsider their rigid adherence to preordained destiny.

[The Calm]

In the tranquil hush of dawn's first light,
Where whispers of freedom dance in flight,
There lies a realm untouched by fate's decree,
A haven where souls can truly be free.

No longer bound by chains of destiny's hold,
No longer forced to follow paths foretold,
In the quiet serenity of the soul's embrace,
We find the courage to carve our own space.

Gone are the days of weathering the storm,
Gone are the nights of feeling forlorn,
For in the calm that reigns supreme,
We discover the power to dream.

To chart our course through uncharted seas,
To chase the echoes of our heart's pleas,
To rise above the tumultuous fray,
And seize the dawn of a brand-new day.

So let us embrace this newfound light,
And banish the shadows that cloud our sight,
For in the stillness of our inner being,
Lies the key to freedom, ever freeing.

Epilogue: Acknowledged

In the quiet moments that followed the chaos, a sense of introspection settled over the Island and its inhabitants. The tumultuous events had catalyzed change, prompting a reevaluation of the longstanding tensions between the Island and the surface world. As the dust settled, bridges were tentatively extended, and conversations that had once been fraught with suspicion now flowed with a newfound sense of openness and understanding.

As the communities on the Island and the surface world embarked on the journey toward reconciliation, they found that collaboration was not only beneficial but necessary for their mutual well-being. Once closed off due to mistrust and animosity, trade routes were reopened, allowing for the exchange of goods, resources, and ideas. This economic interdependence fostered a sense of interconnectedness between the two worlds as individuals on both sides realized the tangible benefits of cooperation.

Cultural exchanges played a crucial role in breaking down barriers and fostering empathy between the residents of the Island and the surface world. Festivals, celebrations, and artistic performances became platforms for showcasing the rich diversity of each community's heritage and traditions. Through these shared experiences, people began to appreciate the beauty and uniqueness of each other's cultures, laying the groundwork for mutual respect and understanding.

Perhaps most importantly, shared challenges and triumphs catalyzed the forging of new bonds between the Island and the surface world. Natural disasters, economic hardships, and other crises transcended the boundaries of geography, equally affecting communities on both sides. In times of adversity, individuals came together to provide support and assistance, recognizing that their destinies were intertwined and that unity was essential for overcoming obstacles.

Leaders from the Island and the surface world played a pivotal role in facilitating this spirit of collaboration. Through diplomacy, dialogue, and compromise, they worked tirelessly to address longstanding grievances and build trust between their communities. Their efforts were sometimes resisted, but their unwavering commitment to peace and cooperation prevailed.

The journey toward reconciliation was gradual and multifaceted, marked by moments of progress and setbacks. However, through the collective efforts of individuals on both sides, the once-distant relationship between the Island and the surface world transformed into mutual respect, cooperation, and shared prosperity.

Leaders on both sides played a pivotal role in fostering this spirit of cooperation. Tiriaq and Ayuka, having earned the trust and respect of their people through their courage and leadership, worked tirelessly to bridge the gap between the two worlds. Their efforts were met with cautious optimism, as individuals from all walks of life dared to believe in the possibility of a future where differences were celebrated rather than feared.

Amidst the ongoing efforts towards reconciliation, there were inevitably challenges and setbacks. Old wounds ran deep, and the scars of past conflicts lingered in the collective memory of both societies. Yet, with each passing day, progress was made, however incremental it may have seemed. It was a journey fraught with uncertainty but promised a brighter tomorrow for all who called the Island and the surface world home.

As revered leaders of their respective communities, Tiriaq and Ayuka stood as symbols of hope and resilience in the wake of the unfolding tumultuous events. Their journey of self-discovery and enlightenment transformed them and empowered them to guide their people through profound change.

With the wisdom gained from their trials and the guidance of the Divine Lion still resonating within them, Tiriaq and Ayuka approached their leadership roles with humility and determination. They understood the importance of acknowledging the complexities of their world and fostering inclusivity and understanding among their people.

Tiriaq and Ayuka worked tirelessly to bridge the divide between the Island and the surface world, recognizing that true unity could only be achieved through mutual respect and cooperation. They led by example, demonstrating empathy, compassion, and a willingness to listen to differing perspectives.

Their leadership extended beyond mere governance; it encompassed a vision for a future where all beings' inherent worth and dignity were recognized and celebrated. They championed initiatives to promote equality, justice, and sustainability, laying the groundwork for a society built on principles of harmony and balance.

Despite their challenges, Tiriaq and Ayuka remained steadfast in their commitment to creating a better world for future generations. They drew strength from the lessons of their journey, knowing that the path to lasting change was often fraught with obstacles but ultimately worth pursuing.

As they looked to the horizon, hopeful and determined, Tiriaq and Ayuka knew their work was far from over. But with the support of their people and the legacy of the Divine Lion guiding their steps, they faced the future with unwavering resolve, ready to continue the journey toward peace, unity, and understanding.

Under the guidance of Tiriaq and Ayuka, the Island experienced a renaissance, with prosperity and tranquility spreading across its once-troubled landscapes. A commitment to reconciliation and understanding marked their leadership as they worked tirelessly to heal the wounds of past conflicts and build a more inclusive and compassionate society.

Communities that had once been divided by mistrust and animosity now came together in a spirit of collaboration and mutual respect. Old grievances were set aside as people from all walks of life embraced the shared values of peace, unity, and cooperation. Through dialogue and empathy, Tiriaq and Ayuka fostered an environment where differences were celebrated rather than feared, laying the foundation for a more harmonious future.

As the Island flourished under their stewardship, its inhabitants found renewed hope and purpose in their daily lives. Trade flourished, cultural exchanges thrived, and friendships formed across previously entrenched divides. The scars of old conflicts gradually faded into distant memories, replaced by a sense of optimism and possibility for the future.

A deep commitment to justice and equality characterized Tiriaq and Ayuka's leadership. They implemented policies to address systemic injustices and ensure that every individual had the opportunity to thrive. Through education, empowerment, and advocacy, they sought to create a society where everyone felt valued and respected.

As the Island blossomed under their guidance, the whispers of peace and unity grew louder, echoing through the hearts and minds of its inhabitants. It was a testament to the transformative power of leadership rooted in empathy, compassion, and a steadfast dedication to the common good. As the Island stood on the cusp of a new era of prosperity, Tiriaq and Ayuka looked to the future with hope and optimism, knowing that their journey towards peace and unity was far from over but believing wholeheartedly in the transformative power of collective action and solidarity.

In the realm of endless skies, where stars dance in celestial grace,

Resides the Goddess, with a gentle smile upon her face.

With hands that shape the cosmos, she weaves the threads of fate,

Guiding souls on their journey, through destiny's gate.

Each thread a story, a tale waiting to unfold,

In the tapestry of existence, where wonders are untold.

She spins the fabric of time with delicate precision,

Crafting paths of purpose, with infinite vision.

From the depths of the ocean to the heights of the sky,
Her touch is felt in every whisper, every sigh.
In the rustle of leaves and the song of the breeze,
Her presence is felt, bringing comfort and ease.

She is the light in the darkness, the beacon in the night,
Guiding lost souls towards the path that's right.
With wisdom beyond measure and compassion pure,
She nurtures the world, making hearts feel secure.

In the quiet moments of reflection, her voice is heard,
A gentle reminder of the beauty in every word.
She whispers of hope in times of despair,
Reminding us that love is always there.

Through trials and tribulations, she remains steadfast,
A guiding force in a world that's vast.
Her love knows no bounds, her grace knows no end,
And with every beat of our hearts, she's there as a
friend.

So let us honor the Goddess, in all her divine glory,
And celebrate her presence in every heartfelt story.
For she is the weaver of fate, the keeper of dreams,
And in her eternal embrace, all is as it seems.

Made in the USA
Columbia, SC
11 April 2024

34136039R00150